The Prince of Tarn

The Prince of Tarn

by Hazel Hutchins
illustrated by Ruth Ohi

Annick Press
Toronto • New York

Annick Press gratefully acknowledges the support of the
Canada Council and the Ontario Arts Council.

The editor would like to thank Daniel K. Grindlay, education consultant.

Cataloguing in Publication Data
Hutchins, H.J. (Hazel J.)
The Prince of Tarn
ISBN 1-55037-439-7 (bound) ISBN 1-55037-438-9 (pbk.)

I. Ohi, Ruth. II. Title.

PS8565.U826P74 1997   jC813'.54 C96-932382-4
PZ7.H87Pr 1997

The art in this book was rendered in pen and ink.
The text was typeset in American Garamond.

Distributed in Canada by: Published in the U.S.A. by Annick Press (U.S.) Ltd.
Firefly Books Ltd.   Distributed in the U.S.A. by:
3680 Victoria Park Avenue   Firefly Books (U.S.) Inc.
Willowdale, ON   P.O. Box 1338
M2H 3K1   Ellicott Station
                           Buffalo, NY 14205

Printed and bound in Canada byWebcom.

Where the
Hill-Giants
Dwell

Findlegate

the ford
of Tarn

Tarn

Southlands

There be
Dragons

— Prince of Tarn —

List of illustrations

 Chapter One

$\mathcal{T}$he Prince arrived in Fred's bedroom on May 17ᵗʰ at twelve minutes before midnight.

Fred was asleep. He had just turned eleven that day. His stomach was full of his father's half-cooked cake and his dreams were full of all the things that might have been but weren't. And in the midst of this he heard,

"You there, like a great lump in the bed, wake up."

and

"How like Ezran to just dump us here without any concern for ceremony."

and

"We'll need food from the kitchens, riding clothes, a loyal escort and the fastest horses in the stable."

There was a thump as a toe was stubbed in the darkness, and a string of curses.

"Giants' teeth! Will someone not fetch a light!"

Fred turned on his bedside lamp. It was just a small lamp, but Fred, being rather small himself, had armed it with a 150-watt bulb. The intruder was blinded. Fred, being behind the lamp, was almost blinded, but not quite.

In a few quick blinks, Fred could see well enough to make out the person standing before him. It was a boy—a tall, slim boy, perhaps a year older than Fred himself. His hair was pulled back in a ponytail at the base of his neck. He wore a long jacket and tight leggings—both of them blue with golden threads that caught the light rather successfully. On his shoulder was embroidered a wonderful eagle whose talons were curved tightly around a golden stick.

With a start, Fred realized he knew that eagle.

"The Prince of Tarn!" said Fred.

"His Royal and Eminent Highness the Prince of Tarn, if you don't mind!" said the Prince, squinting hard into the light. "And shield that torch!"

Fred turned the lamp towards the ceiling. The Prince looked down at Fred sharply.

"Get up. Did you not hear us? Alert the kitchens. Send us the Captain of the Guard and the Stable Master."

Fred did indeed begin scrambling out of bed, although of course there were no kitchens, Captain of the Guard or Stable Master in his apartment.

"But first," said the Prince, putting out a regal arm to bar his way, "where is it that Ezran has sent us? To Tindlegate? If we've been sent all the way to the Southlands we'll..."

Fred ducked under the arm and left the room. He trotted

down the hallway to where his father was snoring peacefully with his head half-buried in his pillow. The small balding spot at the back of his head shone dully in the half-darkness.

"Dad. Dad?" He gave his father's shoulder a shake. His father came awake with a start.

"Fred? What time is it?"

"Midnight," said Fred. "We have to talk."

"Midnight!" said his father. "Fred, midnight is not a good time for talking."

"Dad, I know you think I'm still a little kid, but I'm not. I can't stay little forever just because you want me to. I know you worked really hard on all those teddy bears for my birthday cake, but I'm not four years old any more. I don't need teddy bears. I don't want to go to little-kid movies. And this business with the Prince of Tarn...I know it probably cost a lot to have someone dress up and come in and pretend, but I don't believe in the Prince of Tarn any more. I grew up a long..."

"Fred, what are you talking about?"

"He looks great. He looks just like he did in the book and he talks just right too—all royal-sounding and saying 'we' instead of 'I'. But I'm not little any more...I'm..."

"Who looks great?"

"The Prince of Tarn!" said Fred. "The kid in my room dressed up as the Prince of Tarn."

"Here? Now?" asked his dad, struggling to sit up in bed. "Fred, I didn't hire anyone to dress up as the Prince of Tarn."

Fred looked at his dad closely in the semi-darkness. He was

pretty sure his dad was telling the truth. He was the kind of dad who didn't ever tell a joke, let alone a lie. In fact he was so dreadfully serious that sometimes it drove Fred a little nuts.

His father climbed out of bed and pulled on his housecoat. He followed Fred down the hall. Together they peered in at Fred's doorway. The Prince was pacing back and forth.

"We'll have Ezran kicked completely out of the castle this time," he was saying. "Ezran and those wretched owls and..."

Fred ducked out of sight as the Prince turned to the doorway. His father, however, was caught standing in plain view.

"What are you staring at?" demanded the Prince. "If you are the Captain of the Guard or the Stable Master, present yourself properly. If not, go about your business before we see that you have none!"

Fred's father stepped back into the hallway. There was a look of amazement on his face.

"It's incredible," he said. "It's him, right down to the satin slippers and the tone of his voice. He's just the way he should be!" He peered around the corner again and quickly withdrew. "He's wonderful—isn't he wonderful?"

"Well, I guess so," said Fred, "I mean, he's exactly like the Prince would be. But honestly, Dad, that's not..."

"Your mother would have loved to see him," interrupted Fred's father. "He was her favourite, you know—of all the characters in all her books, he was the one..."

"But who is he?" asked Fred.

"The Prince of Tarn," said his father. "You said so yourself."

"He can't be the Prince," said Fred. "There is no real Prince. It's all a story."

His father raised a hand. "Look, Fred, it's hard for you to understand. I know that. You were only five when your mother died, and it's hard for you to remember what she was like. But Fred—she was different. She could see things and do things and understand things that normal people couldn't. I've told you how things were in this room when she used to write in here. How mist used to leak from under the doorway. And the smell of cooking. And the noise of sword fights."

"But you were just making those things up!" said Fred.

His father shook his head. Fred opened his mouth and closed it several times. He looked at his father hard. Was he beginning to crack up? Everything felt all weird.

"I really, truly didn't hire him," Fred's dad was saying. "And you didn't hire him. Who else knows about the Prince of Tarn? The book was never published. Your mom never even sent it around." His father looked at Fred for a moment. "If you're scared, you needn't be. Nothing from your mom's stories would ever hurt you."

"I'm not scared!" said Fred.

"You'll be scared shortly," said the Prince, stepping into the hallway. "A simple request—food, horses, clothing—and here you are dithering. Both of you! We believe we've landed in a nest of dolts! Where is the Captain of the Guard?"

The Prince turned regally and took off down the hallway.

"Guards! Guards!" he called.

Fred and his father followed him into the kitchen. The

bedroom light seeped down the hall and turned the small area into shades of grey. It was impeccably neat—the way Fred's father always left a room.

The Prince looked around, spotted the front door and crossed to it. He turned and addressed Fred with mocking politeness. "The passage to your Great Hall? Would it be this way?"

Fred didn't know what to say.

"We wish you to open it," demanded the Prince.

Fred looked at his father. The Prince took a great breath.

"Guards!" he shouted.

At that moment the telephone rang. Fred and his dad both knew who it was.

Fred's father picked it up. He apologized to Mrs. Tobias for the noise. He promised to turn down the television. He hung up. The Prince was watching him suspiciously.

"Look...er...Your Royal Highness...there are a few things..." began Fred's father.

"We wish to go to your Great Hall," said the Prince loudly. "We wish to go now. We wish this passage opened and..."

"...And the Prince of Tarn always gets his way," said Fred to his dad softly. "If he really is the Prince of Tarn."

Fred and his father looked at each other for a moment. The last thing they needed was one of the Prince's famous temper tantrums, at midnight with Mrs. Tobias already complaining.

Fred crossed to the door and opened it.

"Better," said the Prince. "Much better." He walked out into the hall. Behind him Fred saw his father take his long

15

raincoat from the closet and slip it on. Then he, too, followed.

There were six other apartment doors and an elevator door that opened off the side of the hall, but the Prince ignored them. He walked down the length of the hall and through the doorway at the end.

Here, it seemed to Fred, he stopped for a moment. Perhaps he was surprised at finding himself in a stairwell instead of some large connecting passageway. The sound of voices rising up the stairwell, however, seemed to give him direction.

He descended very grandly, looking straight ahead. His slippers reached regally forward and then dropped without a sound into place on the cement steps.

Fred and his father followed. They said not a word. Fred was vaguely aware that he was walking down towards the apartment-house lobby in his pyjamas, following someone dressed as if to go to a masquerade ball, but it didn't seem to be real, somehow. Things rarely seem real when you are woken at midnight from a deep sleep on your eleventh birthday.

Down and down and down. The door between the main lobby and the stairwell had been propped open and the Prince stepped forward onto the carpet. He stood looking around him. He was not pleased.

"This is not a Great Hall," he said.

"That's what I was trying to tell you," began Fred's dad.

The elevator opened and a man stepped out. He gave the Prince a quick look and hurried out the front doors. The Prince strode to the doors and stood expectantly before them.

Fred looked at his father. His father's look was beginning to register alarm, but, like Fred, he didn't seem to know what to do about the situation.

Seeing that neither was about to open the door for him, the Prince gave them a withering look.

"You shall both pay dearly for your insolence," he said.

He pushed first against the inner door and then the outer door. At exactly midnight the Prince of Tarn stepped onto the sidewalk in front of the Winguard apartments.

He stepped out onto the pavement and stopped. On either side of him stretched a broad avenue—cars and lights and neon that seemed to go on forever. Buildings crowded around in the blackness and light. And at that exact moment, as if on cue, a fire engine and two ambulances turned a corner down the street. With sirens blasting and lights strobing the night, they came wailing and flashing like terror itself down the avenue towards them.

The Prince froze. All colour drained from his face. His eyes were larger than Fred had thought anyone's eyes could be.

The ambulances and fire engine passed in a great, noisy, brilliant rush. The Prince stared and stared as they fled into the distance. Then, slowly, he began to breathe again. He began to breathe, but not too deeply. He turned.

"We shall now return to our rooms," he said stiffly, but with dignity.

Fred, who had begun to feel very strange standing on the avenue in his pyjamas, jumped to open the door for him. The Prince entered the lobby and made for the stairwell.

When they reached the fifteenth floor, Fred's father was standing waiting for them. Fred was not surprised. His father hated climbing stairs and had obviously taken the elevator. The Prince frowned, but said nothing. He walked right by him and down the hall. He looked like he was going to keep walking forever, so Fred whispered, "Fifteen-oh-nine. On the front of the door."

The Prince stopped before the door marked 1509.

Fred's dad opened it. The Prince stepped through. He walked through the kitchen and down the hall and back into Fred's bedroom. He stood where he had first appeared, in the middle of the room on the old patched quilt that was always falling out of Fred's closet.

"Ezran, you have gone too far this time," said the Prince in a loud voice. "We insist on being returned to Tarn this moment. We order you. We command you. We shall not move from this spot until we are standing in the very centre of the Great Hall of Tarn, where we belong. We take that as a sacred vow."

He stood utterly upright and utterly rigid and utterly unmoving.

Fred and his father watched him for some time. At last Fred's dad motioned Fred out into the hallway.

"Knowing what we do about the Prince of Tarn and his sacred vows, and knowing how stubborn Ezran is in the stories, I'd say the Prince is going to be standing there awhile. How about grabbing your blankets and coming into my room for the night?"

"And just leave him here?" asked Fred.

"He's exactly where he should be," said Fred's father. "He'll be gone by morning."

Fred looked at the Prince.

"When he really does disappear, I'd like to see it," said Fred.

His father hesitated.

"I'll be all right," said Fred. "You said so yourself."

Fred's dad nodded. He said good night and went off to his room. Fred wrapped his comforter tightly around himself and curled up on the far corner of his bed. He looked at the Prince. Bits and scraps of the old story came tumbling through his head.

The Prince of Tarn, the most spoiled prince in all the kingdoms.

The Prince of Tarn who always got his own way.

The Prince of Tarn who teased the swans in the moat, stole the wizard's golden staff and played tricks on everyone without once being punished.

The Prince of Tarn who...who what? He didn't know why he was bothering sitting here. It was all just a story. A stupid little kids' story. Stories had nothing to do with real life—Fred had figured that out a long time ago.

An emptiness settled upon Fred. He didn't know where it came from, but he'd felt it more and more lately. What did it matter anyway? What did anything matter?

Fred's head began to nod. His breathing began to lengthen. It was not long before his chin settled on his chest and he began to sleep in fits and starts.

And although he heard a dull thump sometime around four in the morning, he did not waken.

 Chapter Two

"Brring. Brring. Brring..."

Fred jumped out of bed, leapt over something on the floor, rounded the corner into the hallway and managed to pick up the telephone on its fourth ring.

"I don't hear any movement over there. You're late," said Mrs. Tobias, and the line went dead.

Fred looked at the clock on the living-room wall.

"Daaaaad!" he called, racing down the hall.

His father stuck his head out of the bathroom. He'd already finished brushing his teeth.

"I heard the phone," he said. "What a morning to be late. I've got meetings all day. And you'll have to get moving yourself."

"Right," said Fred and headed back to his bedroom. Ten seconds later he was back. "What about the Prince?"

His dad was pulling on his pants. He stopped with one leg

in and one leg out. He looked sideways at Fred.

"A dream," he said.

Fred took off down the hall. Someone down the hall said, "Youch!" A moment later Fred was back. His dad was buttoning his shirt and pulling the bedclothes together at the same time. Even when he was in a hurry he wasn't about to leave the bed unmade.

"Do dreams shout when you pinch them?" Fred asked.

Fred's father stepped into his shoes, grabbed his tie and followed Fred down the hall.

The Prince of Tarn was sitting in the middle of Fred's bedroom. He was rubbing the sleep from his eyes and scowling.

Fred's dad actually smiled at the sight. "'The Prince of Tarn always awoke with a scowl on his face,'" he said.

Fred recognized it as a quotation from the story.

"He shouldn't be here," he said.

"No, he shouldn't," said his father. His smile faded. "I don't know what we're going to do." He stepped back into the hall, took a deep breath and ran his fingers through his hair. "Fred, you're going to have to take care of him."

"Take care of him!" said Fred.

"Yes, you'll have to take care of him," said his dad. "You saw him last night. He doesn't know where he is. He can't be left on his own. Take him to school with you and..."

"Take him to school with me?! I can't take him to school with me! What'll everybody think? It'll be like taking some nursery-rhyme character to school. In grade five for crying out

22

loud. I'll be slaughtered if they believe me, which they won't, because they'll just think I'm plain nuts, which is just as bad. And you saw what he was wearing!"

"Find him some clothes and take him to school with you. I'll write your teacher a note saying he's a cousin visiting from ...from out in the country somewhere...and he wants to see what our schools are like. They let people do that."

He strode quickly out to the kitchen and began scribbling on the pad on the table.

"Can't he just stay here in the apartment?" asked Fred.

"No, he's liable to take off and get into trouble. You know what he's like," said Fred's father.

"Then I'll just stay home with him," said Fred.

His father looked at him sternly. "You could have stayed home with him if you hadn't played hookey six times last month. No. You have to go to class. That was the deal we made."

At the mention of the words "the deal" Fred knew he'd lost the argument.

"I've got to get going, and so do you," said his father. "You've got ten minutes before Rebecca gets here."

"What will I tell Rebecca?"

"Same thing as the teacher, I guess. Make it up as you go along. Just keep an eye on him until he...goes back where he came from."

He grabbed his briefcase and jacket, gave Fred a quick hug and looked over his shoulder.

"The Prince of Tarn..." he said. For the briefest of moments the words hung in the air like a talisman, a magical charm. And then he was gone.

Fred stood in the kitchen, staring at the door. How could his dad do this to him? He tried to think very hard. He'd never had an imaginary person in his bedroom before, let alone been told to take care of one. He stood there waiting for some sort of voice to speak in his head and tell him what to do.

No voice spoke. The longer he stood there, however, the more certain he was that he couldn't take the Prince of Tarn to school. Fred had a hard enough time surviving at school as it was.

Fred thought of what his father had said. He was to keep the Prince safe. He wasn't to stay home with him. Surely that left some room for manoeuvring, if he was careful.

"Servant. Servant!"

Fred went down the hall to his bedroom. The Prince had installed himself in the middle of the bed. He had tucked Fred's favourite pillow behind his head and plumped Fred's favourite comforter all around him. Fred's comic books had been strewn across the floor.

"We shall have breakfast before we rise—pheasant, strawberries and isle cakes," he announced.

Fred scowled, but he went back to the kitchen. If a prince had appeared in his bedroom, maybe pheasant, strawberries and isle cakes—whatever they were—had appeared in his fridge. Fred opened the door. Inside were two oranges and a slice of three-day-old pizza. Fred had been saving the pizza for his breakfast.

Smack. Smack. Smack. Mrs. Tobias was rapping on the wall. Now that she'd heard his dad leave the apartment, Fred knew, she'd knock every thirty seconds until she heard Fred running water in the bathroom. Mrs. Tobias drove him nuts.

Then, suddenly, an idea began forming in Fred's head. It had to do with the way the lock jammed on the bathroom door. It had gotten so bad, in fact, that if you locked yourself in by accident you had to be rescued by someone on the hall side using the short, stiff length of wire Fred's dad kept taped above the doorway just in case.

Fred threw the oranges on a plate, added the pizza in a sudden mood of generosity, and hurried down to the Prince.

"This is all we have," he said.

The Prince picked the pizza up, gingerly, by his fingertips. He nibbled at one edge. He nibbled at the other. And then, as Fred watched, he wolfed the remainder down in two bites.

"Look," said Fred, and if he sounded a bit short it was probably because of the speed at which his pizza had disappeared, "I've got something important to show you."

"We require a finger bowl," said the Prince, waving his sticky fingers. "Then we shall require the royal dressers and some sort of amusement to pass the time till lunch—jugglers would do."

Fred forced a smile onto his face. After all, the Prince had actually played right into his hands.

"Your Highness," said Fred. "In the Winguard apartments we do not have finger bowls. We do, however, have something far better. We have an entire room devoted to Your Highness's convenience. This way, your Most Royal and Noble Highness."

It was exactly how the Prince liked to be addressed. He followed Fred down the hall.

Rebecca arrived six minutes later. Fred was dressed and ready for school. He even had his books waiting by the door.

"I can't believe it!" said Rebecca. Her green eyes loomed large behind the rims of her glasses and her coppery hair crackled with early morning static. "You're ready on time! But why is your dad still here?"

"He's not," said Fred.

"What's the banging down in the bathroom?" asked Rebecca.

"Hot water pipes," said Fred, pushing her out the door. "Come on. We're going to be late."

 Chapter Three

$\mathcal{A}$t school that morning, Fred was pleased to find that he didn't feel even a little bit guilty about having locked the Prince in the bathroom. All he felt was relief—relief that he didn't have a fairy tale following around after him. And if what his dad said was true, the Prince would be gone entirely by the time school was over and the problem would be solved.

He set his mind into neutral and pretended to be listening to the teacher. It was a trick he'd been using more and more lately—being there and not being there all at once. It helped to ease something inside him.

Whap. Something small and wet smacked against Fred's left ear.

Fred turned his head a half notch.

Whap. Something hit him on the cheek.

Jammy Murdock was sending spitballs his way. Big, gobby, wet spitballs, as only Jammy Murdock could send.

Fred scowled at him. Not only was school itself hard to take, but you could also look forward to being bugged—even by your friends. And his father wondered why he liked to stay home and watch television some days.

Recess wasn't much better. Recess was the time when they almost let you go, but not quite. Some kids, Fred knew, actually liked recess. They liked to wrestle or play ball or just bug people. At recess Fred walked around the playground trying to stay out of trouble. Jammy Murdock walked with him.

"I make good spitballs, hey," said Jammy Murdock.

Fred didn't answer.

"Why did you walk to school with Rebecca this morning?" asked Jammy.

"I always walk to school with Rebecca," said Fred. "My dad's made me walk to school with Rebecca since I was six years old."

"Why does he make you?" asked Jammy.

"Because he does," said Fred.

"Are you in love with her?" asked Jammy.

"No. I told you, my dad makes me," said Fred.

"But why her?" asked Jammy.

"She lives in the same apartment building," said Fred.

"Weren't her mom and your mom friends?" asked Jammy.

"Yes," said Fred.

"How can they be friends if your mom's dead?" asked Jammy.

"They *were* friends. When Rebecca and I were little. Jammy, you know all this."

"But why do you always have to walk to school with her?" said Jammy.

Fred wondered for about the thousandth time what he was doing with a friend like Jammy Murdock.

"Fred. Freeeed!"

Rebecca came running across the playground. "We've got to go back to your apartment. Mrs. Tobias phoned the office. There's water leaking out of your apartment into the one below. Your dad must have left the shower on." Rebecca suddenly turned white. "Or maybe he didn't leave, after all. Maybe he had a heart attack and is lying there helpless. Come on!"

"No!" said Fred.

"What do you mean, no!" said Rebecca. "Your dad could be dying!"

"I mean...I mean, wait!" said Fred. "You stay here and tell Ms. Nicks about what's happened and I'll go home and..."

But Rebecca was pulling on his arm, convinced that his father was in mortal danger.

"Ms. Nicks already knows. She's the one who sent me to get you. Fred, we've got to hurry. Come on!"

She dragged Fred across the playground in front of Jammy Murdock and anyone else in elementary school who happened to look their way.

Mrs. Tobias was waiting by the door of Fred's apartment. Her hair was orange this week. She was wearing a house dress with large parrots printed all over it in bright colours. On her feet were the flip-flop sandals she wore summer and winter.

Around her neck were pieces of cork strung together with wooden sticks—one of her never-ending craft projects.

"It's a good thing I know where you go to school," said Mrs. Tobias. "The caretaker's out. Who knows how much damage has been done."

Fred unlocked the door. Both Rebecca and Mrs. Tobias pushed close to follow him.

"You better wait here," he told them. "In case you get washed away or something."

He slipped through the door, locked it behind him and quickly headed down the hall. He could hear the noise of running water, and outside the bathroom the carpet was sopping wet.

"Your Highness—turn off the water!" called Fred.

No answer, and the water kept running. Fred began to feel uneasy.

He reached above the door for the length of wire, inserted it into the little hole in the doorknob and wiggled it until the pin sprang free.

The bathroom was in flood. All taps were open and towels were plugging the drain-holes. The room simply overflowed with water. Perched on the tank behind the toilet was the Prince. The self-satisfied look on his face wiped away any feeling of relief Fred might have had at seeing him there.

"I showed you how to turn off the taps!" said Fred angrily. "You did this on purpose!"

The Prince allowed the corners of his mouth to rise slightly in a very superior smile.

"Who's that, Fred?"

Fred spun around. Rebecca was standing at his shoulder. Too late, he remembered that she had her own key. Fred took a quick look down the hall behind her. At least she hadn't let Mrs. Tobias in with her.

"Well? Who is it?" asked Rebecca. "And don't tell me it's one of your relatives, because I know you don't have any—not that your dad will admit to, anyway. Who is it?"

Fred sighed miserably. "The Prince of Tarn," he said. And wading into the bathroom he began to turn off the taps.

 Chapter Four

"It's really him!" said Rebecca.

Fred was lying on the living-room rug, waiting for the wet towels to finish in the dryer and wishing the world would go away. The Prince was in Fred's bedroom, going through another session of unsuccessfully ordering Ezran to bring him home. Rebecca was sitting on the sofa with a book in her hands. Although she'd found it on the same shelf as the published books Fred's mother had written, this one was very different. It was a slim book with a soft brown leather cover. Only one copy existed and it had been made for Fred by his mother's hands alone. It was titled *The Prince of Tarn*.

"Look at the eyes! And the expression! He's the same! Except he's a lot younger in the book than he is now."

Fred hadn't thought of that before. In the book the Prince had only been six or seven. How could a fairy-tale character grow up?

Rebecca was turning pages. Fred caught glimpses of pictures he hadn't seen in a long time. There was a small boy, dressed in pale blue, standing beside a swan-filled moat. There was a golden staff and a puff of smoke.

"Did your mother do all the hand-lettering? And all the drawings?" asked Rebecca.

Fred nodded.

"There's castles and dungeons, horses and dragons and giants. What are these trees? Almost every page has one or two along the edge somewhere. They're beautifully wild- and mysterious-looking. Is there something special about them?"

"I don't remember any trees," said Fred, "except that my mom used to doodle them while she was thinking."

"Who's this person standing on the turret, in the long robes?" asked Rebecca.

"Ezran. The wizard," said Fred.

"A wizard? I always like stories with wizards."

"Whenever the Prince gets into a scrape, the wizard rescues him in some magical way," said Fred. "Or else it's some poor ordinary person that Ezran has to rescue because the Prince has had a temper tantrum. That's how the stories go. It's pretty babyish, really."

"I thought you said it was wonderful," said Rebecca.

"I said I thought it was wonderful when I was little," said Fred. "And when it was in a book. That doesn't mean it's wonderful in my apartment when I'm eleven years old."

"Why not?" asked Rebecca.

"Because it isn't," said Fred.

Rebecca looked at him in a funny way, then turned back to the book in her hands.

"This Ezran-wizard-person is the one the Prince was yelling at in the bedroom," said Rebecca. "I wonder why?"

"Servants do not wonder about princes," said the Prince himself, striding into the living room. "And they do not talk behind the royal back."

He walked across the carpet, did a dramatic turn, and paced back again.

"We aren't exactly servants," said Rebecca.

The Prince stopped in mid-stride and raised a questioning eyebrow.

"What are you?" he asked.

"Just us," said Rebecca. "Rebecca and Fred. We live here; that is, Fred lives here. I live one floor up."

"Then we suppose you are commoners as opposed to servants. And in that case we shall ask you a question," said the Prince. "How long should it take a wizard to get over the fact that someone released six mice in the castle's dren?"

"A dren?" asked Rebecca.

"A place where a wizard hangs out," said Fred. "And you can bet the Prince is the one who released the mice."

The Prince scowled at Fred, but did not disagree.

"Well," he asked Rebecca, "how long?"

"I don't know much about wizards. It doesn't sound too terrible, though. I mean, a few mice...aren't wizards' places kind of messy anyway?"

"Wonderfully messy," said the Prince.

"Then I don't think it would take very long to get over it at all," said Rebecca.

"Precisely," said the Prince. "So what are we doing here?"

"I came to help Fred," said Rebecca.

"He's using the 'royal' we," said Fred. "He means himself."

"Oh," said Rebecca. She turned back to the Prince. "Has this wizard person ever sent you away before?"

"Once or twice," said the Prince.

"Lots of times," corrected Fred. "To the tops of mountains, deserted islands, a turret or two and..."

"How would you know!" said the Prince. "You're a mere commoner. And if those owls have been spreading stories, let it be known here and now that those mangy feather dusters aren't to be trusted."

"And once to the caves of the gnomelings," finished Fred.

"If you know so much, you will also know that it was only for a few hours, at the most," said the Prince. "This is preposterous. We think perhaps Ezran has grown addle-brained."

"Or else this Ezran person really wants you to learn a lesson this time," said Rebecca.

"A lesson?" asked the Prince.

"That's how a lot of stories seem to go," said Rebecca. "And if you're a charac..."

Fred jumped up, stepped in front of Rebecca and gestured grandly towards the curtains that covered the balcony windows.

"Why don't you look out the window and see what things

look like in the daylight," he told the Prince.

The Prince looked towards the curtains and hesitated. Fred realized that, in spite of all the Prince's bravado, his experience with the fire engine last night had frightened him a good deal.

As if reading his mind, the Prince lifted his chin. "Yes," he said. "We should like to see."

Fred opened the curtains to show the small balcony and the city spread out below it. Because they were on the fifteenth floor, and because they were the only apartment building up on the north edge of town, it was rather a wonderful view, showing both the city and the hills beyond.

The Prince looked very satisfied. Clearly there was no danger. He took several confident steps forward. Crash—he slammed into the glass doors.

Fred heard Rebecca squeak as if she were stifling a laugh. The Prince must have heard it, too, but it was Fred he scowled at.

"We wish to go out on the ledge," he said.

"All right," said Fred. "But don't go leaning over the edge or anything. I'm supposed to take care of you."

Fred opened the sliding doors. The Prince stepped onto the balcony. As soon as his back was to them, Fred turned to Rebecca, took the book from her hands, and hid it beneath a sofa cushion.

"What are you doing, Fred?" asked Rebecca. "Don't you want him to see the book? Doesn't he know he's a story?"

"I don't think so," said Fred, motioning to her to keep her voice down.

"Aren't you going to tell him?" she asked.

"No," said Fred. "And don't you tell him either. Who knows whether he'll go back if he finds out he's a story."

"You don't like him, do you?" asked Rebecca.

"What's there to like?" said Fred.

"I can't believe you, Fred!" said Rebecca. "He came out of a book! Do you know how neat that is? If it was me, I'd at least be excited. Nothing exciting ever happens to me—I keep hoping it will, but it never does—and here you are with a prince who stepped out of a book, and all you can think about is getting him to go back."

The Prince turned and walked back into the apartment, his hand slightly extended to guard against glass. His face was solemn.

"We have pity for you, and admiration, even if you are only commoners," he said. "You live in a terrifying and dangerous time."

"Terrifying and dangerous?" said Rebecca. "Did you see a robbery or something?"

She stepped out on the balcony and looked over the edge. The Prince and Fred joined her. Down below, the regular flow of cars and people made their way along the street.

"Those creatures are truly terrible," said the Prince.

"What creatures?" asked Fred.

"The ones that prowl your streets and devour people," said the Prince. "What awful sights Ezran has sent us to see."

"Those aren't creatures!" said Rebecca.

"They're cars," said Fred. "They're like carriages, but without horses to pull them. People drive them."

The Prince leaned over the balcony again.

"You're sure?" he asked.

"Yes," said Rebecca.

"Cars," said the Prince.

"See, you've already learned something," said Rebecca.

The Prince looked thoughtful. "Perhaps, as you said, that is what is needed," he said. "Ezran is always trying to give us lessons. But we don't suppose this would be enough."

"You could come to school with us this afternoon," said Rebecca.

"Rebecca!"

"Well, he could, Fred," she answered. "No one has to be told he's the Prince or anything."

"You don't know him! He's a spoiled brat. He always gets his way. He expects everyone to wait on him. And I, for one, don't have any magic to bail him out if he gets into trouble."

The Prince cleared his throat and gave Fred a very cold look.

"We have decided. We will go to school with you. The girl shall lead the way. You shall follow after you have visited the kitchens and found us some lunch. What we had for breakfast will do."

"What did you have for breakfast?" asked Rebecca.

"I had nothing," said Fred. "He had pizza."

"If we pool our lunch money we can pick one up on the way," said Rebecca.

"He'll eat it all!" protested Fred. "What'll *we* eat?"

"Come on, Fred. It'll be fun," said Rebecca. "It's like showing someone around from another country. Except he's a real prince."

Fred sighed in resignation. "Well, he's already flooded the place. Who knows what he'll do next? All right, Your Highness. You have to change your clothes."

"We have to," said the Prince. "You're telling the Prince of Tarn what we have to do!"

"You have to," said Fred. "You aren't in Tindlegate or Southlands. You're...well, you're just not, that's all. We don't have princes here."

"None?" asked the Prince of Tarn. "None at all?"

"Some countries, but not here. So you're going to get treated like everyone else. And you've got to look like everyone else. And you've got to stop saying we this and we that and just talk like everyone else, too."

"What a strange, strange place Ezran has sent us," said the Prince. He drew himself up very tall, making it clear that although he was about to drop the royal "we" he was still superior in all ways. "Very well. You may dress me."

Chapter Five

It wasn't easily done. The Prince had never dressed himself before, and Fred wasn't about to do it for him. But, once it was accomplished, he looked almost normal in T-shirt, jeans and sneakers.

He didn't look normal in the elevator. He stood there like the captain of a ship and ordered them to take it up and down and up and down eight times in a row. He wasn't normal on the street, either. Once he'd seen for himself that cars really were under the control of people, and not the other way around, he insisted on walking down the middle of the street. Apparently he had always walked down the middle of the street in Tarn. It took a very close call with a bus to finally convince him to stay on the sidewalk. He walked down the centre of that, too—shouting "Stand aside, stand aside," until Fred said there wouldn't be any pizza for lunch unless he started trying to act like everyone else.

The Prince's eyes narrowed.

"That's not a threat," said Fred. "I'm just trying to help you get along."

"Good," said the Prince. "Because the last person who threatened me is still cleaning the hearthstones in the kitchens with a very small brush."

He gawked at cars, traffic lights and televisions in store windows. He wasn't particularly interested in them—as the Prince of Tarn he was mainly interested in himself—but he gawked just enough to slow them down. He treated the restaurant staff like servants and did not share his lunch. When he finished the last piece he wiped his hands on a napkin and said pointedly to Fred, "This time we shall *not* ask for a finger bowl."

On the way out he picked up the serving tray and tried to walk out the door with it: apparently it was just the right size for playing dunkers on the castle moat. It was all Fred could do to persuade him to put it back before they were all arrested.

Even Rebecca was beginning to see the difficulties of having the Prince of Tarn around by the time they got to class.

"Good luck," she said to Fred as she slipped into her own room across the hall.

Fred's teacher read the note Fred's father had written. "We're always glad to have visitors," she said, smiling at the Prince. "And your name is...?"

"You may address me as His Royal High..." began the Prince.

"Hisroy," interrupted Fred. "We just call him Hisroy."

The Prince looked hard at Fred, but did not speak.

"We are doing math for now, Hisroy," said Ms. Nicks. "Why don't you pull up a chair beside Fred's desk."

This the Prince did, and there, much to Fred's surprise, he sat quietly for the rest of the period. Fred was amazed. When math ended and it was time for free reading, the teacher suggested Fred and his guest might be more comfortable on the oversize pillows by the bookshelves.

The Prince gave a big sigh as he plunked down on the cushions beside Fred.

"School here is every bit as boring as school at home," he said.

"I didn't think princes had to go to school," said Fred.

"Ezran makes me," said the Prince, "every morning. It's three hours of torture. And the time I had the teacher thrown in the dungeon for making a test too hard, Ezran even made me let him go."

Fred wondered what Ms. Nicks would think about being thrown in the dungeon for making a test too hard. At least it explained why things had gone along smoothly so far. The Prince was used to school.

Several students came and took books from the bookshelves. Hisroy frowned as he watched them. The ones who took encyclopædias particularly puzzled the Prince.

"Ezran would have a fit if I went around picking up the sacred texts and carting them around with me," he announced.

"They aren't sacred texts," said Fred. "They're

encyclopædias. And the rest are just books. Some are stories and some are about things we're studying—Canada or trees or railroads. Stuff like that. You can look at them if you want."

The Prince reached out and carefully pulled a book from the shelf.

"*Grogan's Giant*," he read. "You have giants here too, do you? Ours are in the north." He opened the book. "They aren't like these, though. Ours have only two eyes." The Prince pulled another book from the shelf. "*Man on the Moon*," he read. "We have fairy tales about the moons too."

He pulled out a book by Dr. Seuss. Fred wondered whether he'd decide it was fact or fiction. The Prince was too intrigued to comment, however, and was soon working his way through all the books on the shelf.

When the recess bell rang, there were twenty-six kids all eager to play with Hisroy. Fred had noticed that about new kids at school. On the first day everyone was their best friend. Since the Prince was used to being in charge, it worked out just right.

"I wish to play that game," he said, pointing to a group of kids playing basketball on the tarmac. "It looks rather like our game of banners."

Because he was new and a visitor, he was let into the game. People even passed him the ball. Fred, who was never invited to play, had to stand on the sidelines.

"Why is he called Hisroy?" asked Jammy, who was standing next to Fred.

"Because it's his name," said Fred.

"I never heard of a name like Hisroy," said Jammy.

"It's his nickname," said Fred.

"Why does he have a nickname?" asked Jammy.

"Because he does," said Fred.

"Yeah, but why is it weird, like Hisroy?" asked Jammy.

Fred sighed.

Rebecca hadn't gone out for recess, but as they came in she was waiting for Fred in the hall.

"How's he doing?" she asked while Hisroy was discovering how to drink from a fountain.

"He's not very good at basketball or drinking from water fountains," said Fred. "Other than that it's okay, except he gets kind of mixed up about what's real and what's not."

"What do you mean?" asked Rebecca.

"You know—things like dragons and giants are real in Tarn, so he thinks they must be real here."

"Has anybody guessed he's—different?" asked Rebecca.

"I don't think so," said Fred.

"Maybe he'll never go back," said Rebecca.

Fred looked startled.

"Ezran always takes him back," he said firmly.

"Ezran always takes us back," repeated the Prince at supper time that evening.

They were eating pizza. Fred's father had brought it home with him after work. This time Fred was finally getting his share.

"But you made out all right at school?" asked Fred's dad.

"It was okay," said Fred. "Ms. Nicks thought it was kind of weird when 'Hisroy' suggested Jammy be thrown in the moat for firing spitballs—but at least it made Jammy stop for a while."

"I like school here as much as I like school in Tarn," said the Prince. "It is a disgusting waste of time. And I do not like the creature next door."

Fred's dad looked at Fred questioningly.

"Mrs. Tobias tried to cut his ponytail," said Fred.

"She what?" asked Fred's father.

"When we came home she was sitting outside her door with a pair of scissors. She offered to give Hisroy a haircut. I don't know how she knew about him. She must have seen us leave at lunch, I guess."

"I don't believe it," said Fred's father.

"Neither did I," said the Prince. "All in all, however, I suppose it has been a very instructive day. It is now over."

The Prince finished his piece of pizza and tucked two more into his pocket. He went down to Fred's bedroom, picked up his own clothes and stood beside the bed.

"There, Ezran. We have been out. We have learned things. We are full to the brim with lessons. Now BRING US HOME!"

Nothing happened.

Fred and his father watched for a few moments longer. They'd seen it all the night before. They went back to finish their pizza.

"It's hard to believe he's still here," said Fred's dad. "But you did a good job of taking care of him. Thank you, Fred."

"It wasn't as bad as I thought it would be," said Fred. "I

just had to kind of be...creative sometimes."

"I know how that is," said Fred's dad. "You should have heard me trying to convince Mrs. Tobias it was a new kind of deodorizer the day the whole floor of this building filled up with the smell of skunk."

"Really?" asked Fred. "Was Mom writing a story with a skunk in it? Did she know what was happening in the apartment?"

"No," said his dad. "I never told her. I never told her any of it. I was afraid that if she knew, it would somehow stop her from being able to write so well."

They were both silent for a moment. Then Fred's father said quietly, "Fred, I've been thinking. I probably shouldn't have stuck you with the Prince. Tomorrow—if he's still here—I'll find some way to look out for him."

"No, I can handle him," said Fred, surprising himself. "Rebecca will help—she's good at bossing people around. Except I'm not sure he'll want to go to school."

"I'll think about that one," said his dad.

A short time later the Prince came out of the bedroom and demanded to be entertained. Fred turned on the television, but the Prince only scowled.

"If I want to be amused by someone else's hallucinations I can always visit the gnomelings' caves—silly creatures that they are," he said. "Do you not have a dragon board?"

Being entertained, it turned out, meant that the Prince wanted to cheat at Black and White Dragons, a game played on a checker board, so he could beat Fred twenty-two times in a row. They were on game number twenty-three when the phone rang.

"Fred?" said Rebecca. "There's something I have to tell you. I didn't tell my mom about Hisroy because you didn't want me to, but I asked her about your mother's imagination. She said strange things used to come out of that room when your mother was writing—wind and smoke and cooking smells and sounds of laughter."

"That's what my dad said. I told you that," said Fred.

"I know. I know. But I don't believe everything you tell me. My mom's a lot more reliable," said Rebecca. "Anyway, I thought you should know, because it's not like you're just imagining the Prince being there. Are you? I mean he didn't just fade away or anything. Did he?"

Fred looked around the corner into the dining room where the Prince was "accidentally" bumping one of Fred's dragon-checkers onto a square that put all Fred's dragons in danger. "He's still here."

Fred hung up the phone. He went back into the dining room. He watched the Prince clear his dragons off the board with one long, self-indulgent move of his hand. It was a relief when Fred heard Mrs. Tobias rapping on the wall.

"Time for bed," said Fred.

He went into the living room. His dad had fallen asleep on the sofa.

"All that dad one does is eat and sleep. Laziest servant I ever saw. I'd get rid of him if I were you," said the Prince.

"I can't get rid of him," said Fred. "He's my father. That's what the word dad means."

"Your father?" The Prince took several steps forward, walked around the sofa and peered closely at the sleeping figure.

"All I have is the wretched wizard Ezran. And you've seen how I am treated!"

"What happened to your mother and father?" asked Fred, who was sure the Prince had had parents in the book, if only in the background.

"They are away," said the Prince. "They have been away for ever so long, although it is hard to tell sometimes, the way Ezran fools with time. You know, sometimes I think there are things that princes are not told."

The Prince looked thoughtful, but only for a moment.

"We are retiring for the night," he announced grandly, and did his processional walk down the hall.

"Dad?" said Fred, shaking him. "Dad, it's time for bed."

That night the Prince once again took over Fred's bed, pillow and comforter. Fred was too tired to argue. He spread the old quilt on the carpet, lay down on it, and wrapped it around him. The quilt was lumpy because of its many patches and re-coverings. Fred could never figure out why someone would patch something so many times, but it had been a family heirloom or something. Except for the lumps, it was almost as good as a sleeping bag.

While Fred was trying to get comfortable, the Prince spoke regally into the darkness.

"We now think we haven't been sent away because of the

mice at all," he pronounced. "We think there must be something special going on—a surprise party for us at the castle, most likely—and Ezran has simply placed us out of the way so everything can be arranged in secret. Tomorrow morning we shall find ourself in the middle of a grand celebration!"

Fred wasn't so sure. As he lay waiting for sleep to come, he went over all the things that had happened that day. There was something Rebecca had said earlier in the day, something small, that was niggling at the back of his mind. It still hadn't come to him when he fell asleep and began to dream—a deep, dark dream, of castles and princes and, pushing through the dream itself, his mother's delicate, twisting trees.

Chapter Six

First thing the next morning, Fred got out of bed and padded quietly into the living room. He retrieved the Prince of Tarn book from its hiding place under the sofa cushions. He had only looked at it long enough to confirm that there were indeed trees along the margins, and more than just a few of them, when he heard a wham in his bedroom. He quickly hid the book again and hurried back down the hall.

The Prince was sitting upright in bed with his morning scowl on his face. Several feathers were still floating in the air where he had thrown Fred's pillow hard against the opposite wall.

"I am still here!" announced the Prince disgustedly.

"It's not my pillow's fault," said Fred. "You don't have to go knocking the stuffing out of it!"

"I shall knock the stuffing out of all the pillows I like," said the Prince. "I shall order new pillows and knock the stuffing out of them, too, if I wish! I am the Prince! And I am going to knock the stuffing out of Ezran when I get back to Tarn."

Fred's dad appeared in the doorway. He crossed the room, picked up the pillow, fluffed it a bit and handed it to Fred.

"I have a proposition for both of you," he said. "If His Royal Highness will attend school today—and not knock the stuffing out of anything or anybody—I will pick you both up after school and take you to Landry Park."

The Prince's face instantly brightened. "A swift ride and a hunt on the parklands are just the things I need to clear my thoughts. Call the Falconer and the Stable Master. We shall go there immediately."

"Not the parklands, the park. You still haven't got it yet, have you?" said Fred. "This isn't a castle. There isn't a Falconer or a Stable Master or any servants. And Landry Park isn't that kind of park anyway—it's an amusement park."

The Prince looked at him sideways.

"But you'll like it," said Fred. "The rides are definitely swift—and there's a bit of flying too. There's a roller coaster—a kind of a car on tracks that loops over twice."

"What do you say, Your Highness?" asked Fred's dad.

The Prince gave a single, regal nod of his head. "We shall eat before we rise. Strawberries, pheasant and isle cakes."

Fred went to the kitchen to get leftover pizza.

When Rebecca arrived, Fred told her of the plan for the day.

"It might work," she said. "By the way, Mrs. Tobias stopped me in the hall. She wants to know if the 'peculiar young man with the ponytail is going to lock himself in the bathroom again this morning."

"She really is pretty good at figuring out what's going on over here, isn't she," said Fred.

"Pretty good, but not perfect," said Rebecca. "This is too far-out even for Mrs. Tobias. You better phone her and tell her he's coming to school with us this morning. And I still think we should tell my mom about him too."

Fred sighed. Mrs. Tobias drove him nuts. Rebecca, when she was in one of her bossy moods, drove him nuts too.

"Mrs. Tobias might call the caretaker and complain," said Rebecca. "Call her, Fred."

It was day two for the "new kid at school" and Fred could already see the glow beginning to wear off. Two of the grade sixers tripped Hisroy as he went up the stairs. A little kid laughed at him because he had Fred's T-shirt on inside out. In class, Ms. Nicks had him join in on the spelling test, which she handed back with many small red x's.

Each time the Prince looked knowingly at Fred. As soon as the Prince figured out how he could manage it, the grade sixers, the little kid and Ms. Nicks were all headed for the dungeon.

Recess was hardest of all, however. Where the Prince had been the centre of attention the day before, he was now just another kid. He walked onto the basketball court and announced he was going to play banner ball, but no one passed him the ball. He demanded a chocolate bar from the school store and was told to get lost. When he started to tell a story of how he'd seen two of the hill-giants, everyone just rolled their eyes and walked away.

In the end, the Prince of Tarn was relegated to walking with Fred and Jammy.

"Why is your name Hisroy?" asked Jammy.

The Prince opened his mouth to give his full and glorious title, but Fred caught his eye. The Prince sighed. "Because it is," he answered.

"Yeah, but why?" asked Jammy.

"Just..." He looked at Fred. "...because," he finished.

"If my name was Hisroy, I'd change it. Why don't you change yours?" asked Jammy.

"I do not wish to change it," said the Prince.

"And why do you call basketball banners?" asked Jammy.

"Because," said the Prince.

"He sounds just like you," said Rebecca, who had been walking nearby.

"What do you mean he sounds just like me?" asked Fred.

"You know. Jammy always does that 'whiney why' bit to you. And you always go along with it," said Rebecca.

Fred had always thought the whining was all Jammy's fault. Now, with a sinking feeling, Fred realized he himself had been part of it. And here he was even encouraging the Prince to play along.

It made Fred feel really strange inside. And it didn't seem right. This *was* the Prince of Tarn. He was the same prince who flew falcons and rode horses. He was the same prince who had been turned into animals and transported to mountain tops by Ezran the wizard. He was the same prince who put

rocks in the bottom of the laundry ladies' baskets and made all the children of the court play Snake by Twos with him by royal decree.

Suddenly Fred had an idea. He found three sticks and laid them out on the ground. He raced behind the Prince, tagged him on the right shoulder, shouted "Snake by Twos!" and jumped over the first two sticks.

The Prince looked around in surprise. He hesitated, but only for a moment. He grabbed the first stick, flung it across the playground, tagged Fred on the right shoulder and jumped over the two remaining sticks.

Fred, who had only a vague idea of how to play Snake by Twos, then tagged Jammy.

"No, no, no," said the Prince. "Stick first. If you can't get a stick, you can't tag." He then showed how it was done.

Jammy began to play. The Prince explained the "frozen in place" rule for the third stick. Jammy used the rule to tag Fred again. The Prince explained some more. Rebecca joined in. Pretty soon there were a couple of other kids watching too, then they joined in as well. Soon there was a rollicking game of Snake by Twos being played all across the playground.

By the time the bell rang to end recess, the Prince of Tarn had a loyal following—and not the kind that would turn their backs on him tomorrow. It was such a good game and his own love of it was so infectious that Fred had a feeling they'd be playing it for many recesses to come.

"Why do they call it Snake by Twos?" asked Jammy as they entered the school.

"Because the sticks are snakes and you have to jump two of them to be safe," said Fred.

"Yeah, but why do you have to do that?" asked Jammy.

Fred was about to answer, but Hisroy stepped in.

"Jammy," he said, "Jammy, we do not wish you to whine and ask useless questions any more."

Jammy opened his mouth to ask another question. The Prince raised a regal hand.

"Ever," said the Prince of Tarn.

Jammy walked silently—but quite happily—beside them back to class. Fred looked at the Prince. There was a very royal look on his face.

Fred's father arrived after school to find the four of them—Fred, the Prince, Rebecca and Jammy—waiting on the curb.

"All of you?" asked Fred's dad. "Has everyone cleared it with their parents?"

Fred nodded.

The Prince liked Landry Park as much as Fred thought he might. It wasn't the roller coaster he liked the best, however. It wasn't even the Ferris wheel or the spinning salt and pepper shakers. In the end it was the swan ride that was his favourite.

Even after Jammy's parents had taken him home, and it was time for the rest of them to leave as well, the Prince insisted on one last ride. Fred and Rebecca climbed in the back seat. The Prince sat alone in the front. He draped one arm over the neck of the mechanical swan as it was pulled through the water, slowly, peacefully on its track.

"Remember the picture in the book?" asked Rebecca. "He's homesick."

"I guess he is," said Fred.

When they returned to the apartment that evening, the Prince seemed to come to some sort of decision. Fred didn't know what he was deciding about, but something was definitely different. He followed purposefully around the kitchen while Fred's father made them a late supper. He was especially interested in the way the stove worked. He even had Fred's dad show him how to boil a pot of water.

His interest did not, however, include washing the dishes when supper was over. Instead he went down to the bedroom in hopes, once again, of being whisked back to his own world. While he was gone Fred opened the small leather-bound book that bore the Prince's name. He turned the pages slowly, one by one, but closed it when his father came into the room. His father looked at him questioningly.

"I was just looking for clues," said Fred. "You know, about how he might get back to Tarn."

"And did you find any?" asked his father.

"Not that I can figure out," said Fred. "It's all..."

"All what, Fred?" asked his dad.

"Nothing," said Fred. "Never mind."

His dad sat down on the sofa. He seemed more relaxed than Fred remembered him being in a long time.

"Do you know what I did today, Fred?" asked his dad. "I left work at lunch, and before I picked you up I drove out to the hills. I went walking where your mom and I used to walk.

I thought I'd never be able to walk there again. But just having the Prince in the house, seeing him and hearing him in all his outrageousness, like a bright spark of imagination...I suppose I thought that was gone forever. It means a great deal to me to know that somewhere that spark still exists."

He looked at Fred. "And it made me realize what a stick-in-the-mud I've become."

"You're not so bad," said Fred. "Just a little...serious."

"And very dull," said his dad. "Teddy bears on your cake! I should have been decorating it with fire-breathing dragons, rockets to the moon..."

"It's okay, Dad," said Fred. "I'm not that kind of kid."

"I'm not so sure," said his dad. "Maybe you've just never had the chance."

Fred looked at the book in his hands.

"I wish there was something more than just this one book," he said. "If I knew more about Tarn, maybe I could understand better why the Prince is here."

"There are other stories," said his dad unexpectedly.

"There are?" asked Fred.

"I'd forgotten, but of course there are," said his dad. "It was a story your mother went back to again and again. There's a whole box of writing about Tarn. It's locked up in our storage area in the basement."

He went to the cupboard and took something from a hook.

"Here's the key to our lock-up. It's too late to get the caretaker tonight, but you can ask him to let you into the basement after school tomorrow."

Fred took the key from his father's hand.

"It's just a box of stories," said his father, "but Fred...be careful. Just in case."

"I'll be careful," said Fred.

That night, when Fred crawled into the quilt on the carpet beside his bed, the Prince again spoke aloud in the darkness.

"We think the commoner Fred may, in time, become an almost passable player of the game of Snake by Twos," he said.

It sounded more like a royal decree than a compliment, but Fred didn't care.

"Thank you," he said.

"And tomorrow," said the Prince, "since Ezran has abandoned me, I shall work on finding my own way home."

Chapter Seven

The next morning, Fred phoned Rebecca and asked her to come down earlier than usual. When she arrived the Prince of Tarn was still breakfasting royally in bed. The pizza had run out and Fred had substituted corn flakes for strawberries, pheasant and isle cakes. The Prince had pronounced them edible—but just barely. Now Fred was having some himself. Rebecca sat down at the table and poured herself a bowl.

"My mom thought it was pretty odd that you asked me to come down early," said Rebecca. "And I guess she ran into Mrs. Tobias, who wanted to know about the ponytail kid. I think she's beginning to suspect something strange is going on."

Fred explained about the box in the basement and the key his dad had given him.

"When do we look—after school today?" asked Rebecca.

Fred didn't know exactly how to say what was going on in

his head. As he was trying to form his thoughts into words, Rebecca jumped to her own conclusions.

"You want to keep it all to yourself, is that it?" she asked. "Wonderful. You tell me about it and then you don't want me to see it. What do you want me to do—keep His Royal Highness entertained while you look?"

Fred was surprised at how angry she seemed.

"It's not fair, Fred," said Rebecca. "Nothing exciting ever happens to me. I always get the dull, responsible jobs—like looking after you. Who's the one that keeps covering for you with Mrs. Tobias? And keeps an eye on both you and the Prince on the playground? Good old reliable Rebecca. I can do other things, you know!"

"Rebecca..." Fred began, but she wasn't about to listen.

"I know you think I'm pretty bossy, Fred," she said. "Maybe I am. But it's just the way I am when people drive me nuts. And I wouldn't have to be bossy if you weren't so..."

"Wimpy?" asked Fred.

"I wasn't going to say that," said Rebecca. "I was going to say mild mannered. That's not so bad. Superman was mild mannered."

"Clark Kent was mild mannered. It's not the same thing."

A funny little twitch played at the corner of Rebecca's mouth.

"Anyway, just because I say things, that doesn't mean that's the way you have to be," said Rebecca. "Or that you have to do what I say. I'd really like to see what's in the box. I could even try not to interfere...too much."

"To tell you the truth, you being bossy isn't what's bothering me," said Fred. "What's bothering me is—what happens if we do find other stories about Tarn? Then what?"

"Well, hopefully, whatever we find out will help Hisroy get home. At least I thought that was the whole idea," said Rebecca.

"I don't think it's as simple as that," said Fred.

"Why not?" asked Rebecca.

Fred fetched the Prince of Tarn book from its hiding place.

"How many trees were there on the pages when you first looked at this?" he asked.

"Trees? Well, there were a few on each page, around the edges. I only noticed them because they were kind of mysterious-looking."

"There's more than just a few around the edges now," said Fred.

Rebecca opened the book. The scattered trees had now become a border on each page—oaks and elms and pine trees, their branches intertwined.

"Are there more than there were before?" asked Fred.

Rebecca nodded.

"And I don't remember any at all," said Fred.

"But you said something about your mom doodling pictures of trees," said Rebecca.

"My dad told me about that," said Fred. "One day when I was having trouble getting ideas for a story for school, Dad said I should doodle, like my mom. He said for her it was a way of easing into her imagination. She'd begin to doodle these tree things and then begin to write, and a story would kind of grow out of the trees."

"But that's not what's happening here," said Rebecca.

"No," said Fred, frowning. He could hear Hisroy coming down the hallway, and he dropped his voice. "I wish I could understand what *is* happening."

That day, the Prince stayed at school without being bribed. For one thing, there was the game of Snakes by Twos to work on. For another thing, he'd found out that the school had a library—an entire room of sacred texts, in the Prince's understanding. The Prince commanded Fred to take him there as soon as possible. Fred had to hurry through his math in order to get some free time. He was surprised to find how quickly he could do his math when he wasn't sitting there spending his time trying not to do it.

"Why did you not bring me here in the first place?" the Prince asked as Fred led him into the large room that served as school library and public library both.

"Shhh," said Fred. "We have to be quiet. I still don't know what you want from here."

"You shall soon find out," said the Prince. "Is that person the Keeper of the Records?"

"Yes, but remember: forget about being royal and all that," said Fred.

The Prince gave him a withering look. He walked boldly up to the librarian. He halted a few steps in front of her. He bared his teeth in what Fred realized was supposed to be a smile.

"If you would be so kind," he said, "we are looking for

sacred texts on the subject of magic. Relocation spells and incantations of travel and destination would be appropriate, but anything close will do."

Fred could have kicked himself. Of course that was what the Prince wanted. He wanted a book of magic spells. He was trying to find out how to get home.

The librarian was looking at Hisroy as if he were crazy.

"It's part of his act," said Fred quickly. "His magician's act. He gets kind of carried away."

"He does, doesn't he?" said the librarian. "Magic is under the 793s."

The Prince raised a haughty eyebrow towards Fred.

"That's the call number, not the number of books about magic," said Fred. "Come on."

He pulled the Prince over to the 793s. There they found three small books and one thicker volume. Fred manoeuvred the Prince to a booth in the farthest corner of the library. The Prince opened up the first one with great reverence and began to read. After a few moments he opened the second book. And then the third and fourth. With each book he opened his face turned redder.

"Rabbits from hats! Scarves that never end! These are not books about magic. These are tricks. Games. Sleights of hand. Is that person trying to make a fool of the Prince? Call the Royal Executioner!"

Fred tried to quiet him. It was pretty embarrassing to be sitting with a raving lunatic in the library, especially when there were bigger kids around. He hustled him out as quickly as he could.

"You should have told me what you wanted," Fred told Hisroy in the hall. "The books in the library are just like in the classroom. Magic isn't a big thing around here. It's not the way our world works."

The Prince glared at him. "Then you live in a very backward world!"

"Look, if it's any help, Rebecca and I are going to look at some things in the basement of our apartment building that may be able to help," said Fred cautiously.

"Are they magic?" asked the Prince.

"No," said Fred.

The Prince threw up his hands in disgust.

"I was brought here by a magic spell," he said. "There will be a counter-spell to take me back. That should be obvious even to you. If you cannot find me books of magic then I shall have to do things another way."

They were outside Fred's classroom. The Prince stopped.

"Aren't you coming back in?" asked Fred.

The Prince shook his head.

"I shall be out on the grounds. I have things to think about."

"But..." began Fred.

The Prince raised a hand. "We shall not be far. We shall cause no trouble. We shall remember we are in disguise."

Fred went back into his classroom. He had things to think about too.

Chapter Eight

When school was over the Prince had done more than think. He had gathered all sorts of sticks, grasses and plant bits from around the neighbourhood. Fred tried not to think about where he'd found the daffodil and iris flowers.

"Let's take the back alleys on the way home," said Rebecca. "Less likelihood of being seen with Joe Florist here."

Fred decided it was one of her better suggestions.

When they reached the apartment building, the caretaker was in the lobby. He was holding wool so Mrs. Tobias could cut it into carefully measured lengths. He looked relieved when Fred and Rebecca asked if he could let them into the storage area in the basement.

Hisroy went along too. While Fred and Rebecca looked at the boxes in Fred's lock-up, the Prince laid out his bits of plants, roots and leaves on an old crate and sorted through them. He lifted each specimen, made a big deal of inspecting it closely, and then laid it down again. The caretaker watched him with great amusement.

There were more boxes than Fred had expected. Fred and Rebecca had to check them out one at a time. Many of them held manuscripts, but none of them was the one for which they were looking.

Hisroy had gathered up his plants and the caretaker was beginning to rattle his keys impatiently when Rebecca spotted one last box that was set on a little ledge at the side.

"That one, Fred," she said.

And, just looking at it, Fred knew she was right. There was something about the way it sat there, its corners softly rounded, the flaps on its lid gently dog-eared. It was a box that had been carefully opened and closed many times. He lifted it down. Written upon it in faded pencil was the word Tarn.

With Rebecca opening doors and the Prince following like a walking garden, Fred carried the box upstairs to his apartment.

"We wish you to call us should anything of importance be found," announced the Prince. He then carried himself and his plants into the kitchen and closed the sliding door.

"What's with him now?" asked Rebecca.

"I don't know, but maybe it's just as well he's out of our hair," said Fred.

He set the box down in the middle of the living room and opened it. Inside was a typed, yellowed manuscript. Beneath it were several coil notebooks, a file folder of loose papers and, in the very bottom, a white plastic pen. The title on the manuscript was the same as had been written on the outside of the box—Tarn. Rebecca carefully picked it up and read the first line.

"It was a magic, waiting to happen." She looked at Fred and smiled. "I like good opening lines," she said.

She began to read again, but her voice quickly trailed off. At first Fred read over her shoulder, but she was a fast reader and soon outdistanced him, turning pages before he was even halfway through. Fred could have said something about bossy people taking over even when they said they wouldn't, but the coil notebooks caught his eye.

He took them over by the window and opened the first one. Almost at once a feeling overwhelmed him, a feeling like all his bones were turning soft and he just might slide away. He looked across at Rebecca. Luckily, she didn't seem to be noticing him. He looked back at the written page.

It was the handwriting that was making him feel so queer. His mother's handwriting. He'd seen it once or twice before, on the inside cover of a book or the back of a photograph. Here, however, it flowed across the page like a great ocean, an ocean that seemed for the first few moments about to sweep him away. It was so much more personal than the typeset of the books on the shelves or even the hand lettering in which *The Prince of Tarn* was written.

Fred sat very still for a few moments, just letting himself become accustomed to the form and shape of the ink upon the page. And then he began to read.

The notes on the pages were far from organized; in fact, they seemed to jump back and forth from one area to another as do thoughts themselves. One page looked like an outline for one of the chapters. Another was a bit of description of Tarn. A third had a sketch of a young woman standing at a parapet. On the page opposite was a hastily scribbled grocery list. "Raisins" was written in large letters. Fred had liked raisins a lot when he was little.

Fred stopped reading and let his eyes wander to the window. Beyond the city he could see the hills where his dad remembered walking with his mom. Here in the apartment, memories were rising around Fred too. There was a worn pair of black beaded slippers that had touched the floor of his bedroom softly, softly. He remembered a green robe that was wonderfully smooth to the touch. A scrap of a song circled around him, the way it might be sung on a grey winter morning. And there was the smell of soap and roses twined together like...

Good grief. Something in the apartment really was beginning to smell. Fred went and stuck his head in the kitchen. The Prince was cooking up a storm and muttering what Fred suspected were magic words under his breath.

"Don't tell me," said Fred. "Magic spells and travel potions, right?"

"Ezran does them all the time," said the Prince. "Nothing to it, really."

"Don't eat anything," said Fred. "And don't burn the place down."

"I know what I am doing," replied the Prince. "I supervised your father with supper last night while you were doing the gnomeling thing."

"Television," said Fred. "It's called television. It has nothing to do with gnomelings."

"Whatever," said the Prince, and turned his back on Fred.

Fred went back to the living room. Once again, as he began to leaf through the coil notebooks, small memories came quietly to greet him. Fred had thought he had forgotten everything about when he'd been little—but it wasn't true.

After a while Rebecca said, "Well, that's it."

"Have you found something? Is it about the Prince?" asked Fred.

"I've found lots of things—it's a wonderful story, Fred—but it's not about the Prince. It's about Tarn itself.

"There were two fortresses—Tindlegate and Southlands," explained Rebecca. "They were nasty places, both of them. They were always fighting and going to wars and throwing people in dungeons. One day the Queen's personal maid from Tindlegate and a stableboy from Southlands fell in love. They were forbidden to see each other, but they ran away and were married by a wizard by a small lake—a tarn."

"How can you read so much so fast?" said Fred.

"I can't," admitted Rebecca. "I found a kind of an outline. I read a bit and look at the outline a bit and it all kind of comes together.

"They decided to live near the lake," continued Rebecca, "and the people of Tindlegate and Southlands began to gather there too. The common people who were sick of fighting and artisans who were sick of building swords and armour came. The servants ran away and came. Gradually even some of the nobility came as well. They all—well, they began to build a fortress themselves—only a different kind of fortress. They built a fortress where people could come when they didn't want to fight. And people did come. It all grew larger, richer and beautiful, too, with farmlands and orchards and gardens and a magic all its own. It was famous for hundreds of miles around. And when the maid and the stableboy had their first child, the people proclaimed themselves a kingdom and declared the child..."

"The Prince of Tarn," said Fred.

"That's right. From the list of presents they brought him, everyone in the whole kingdom began spoiling him right off the bat. I suppose that's why he turned out the way he did— I mean, let's face it, he doesn't exactly fit into the picture as the perfect prince for a place like Tarn—although the story doesn't go that far."

"What do you mean, it doesn't go that far?" asked Fred.

"That's all there is. End of story," said Rebecca.

"It can't be," said Fred.

"That's it," said Rebecca. "The story ends when the Prince is born. Then you've got the Prince of Tarn stories she wrote for you..."

"But there has to be more," said Fred. "You said it yourself: the Prince isn't six or seven any more. He can't have grown older unless my mom wrote him that way."

"Why not?" asked Rebecca.

"Because he's a book," said Fred.

"But that's the way books are, the really good ones," said Rebecca. "When you finish a story, you don't think of everything in the book coming to a great halt. You kind of imagine it going on and on—you just can't watch it happening any more."

"But what about the trees?" asked Fred.

"What?" said Rebecca.

"The trees all around the border of the book," said Fred.

"There aren't any here," said Rebecca. "It's all typewritten, and there aren't any illustrations or doodles or anything. Fred, do you really think the trees have something to do with it?"

"I don't know," said Fred. "It's just that..."

Suddenly the door between the kitchen and the living room flew open. The Prince came out, coughing and sputtering in a great cloud of foul-smelling smoke. The smoke detector began to howl and at the same time the telephone began to ring.

"Quick, you get the stove," said Rebecca. "I'll open the windows."

Fred raced to turn off the stove. He doused the pot under a running tap in the sink. Rebecca fanned the smoke away from the fire detector. The telephone was still ringing.

The Prince did nothing but stand in the middle of the room recovering his dignity. When he seemed to have it well in hand, he sniffed the air experimentally, as if the smell were not a heavy stench at all, but a gentle aroma.

"There is a travel potion that smells very much like this," said the Prince. "We expect we are very close. We shall require some beakers and some better ingredients. Mistletoe. Nightshade. Something to do with bats—dried dung, I think it is."

The line about the smell resembling a travel potion was so obviously a lie and the smell was so very terrible and the mess in the kitchen was so great and Mrs. Tobias, it was now clear, was going to ring that telephone right off the wall if someone didn't pick it up and the demand for dried bat's dung was so ridiculous that Fred exploded.

"No more!" he said. "No more travel potions. No more spells. No bat dung or mistletoe or nightshade. For that matter, no more breakfasts in bed or pulling up other people's gardens or acting so snooty no one can stand you!"

The Prince looked aghast at Fred.

"I mean it. I've had it. NO MORE!"

The Prince straightened his back and raised his chin and looked down at Fred as if from a very great height. He turned on the spot, walked down the hall to the bedroom and slammed the door.

The phone was on its hundred and twenty-fourth ring. Fred picked it up.

"Joe's Pizza," he said. "What-d-ya-want?"

A dial tone buzzed placidly in his ear.

Fred looked at Rebecca. "I've wanted to do that as long as I can remember, and when I finally get the nerve, she's already hung up!"

Fred was dead serious, but Rebecca began to laugh. She laughed and laughed. It was the kind of a laugh people are infected with when things become really absurd. Pretty soon Fred was laughing too.

Together they cleaned up the kitchen. They went through the rest of the papers in the box. There was all sorts of information—maps of Tarn, details of speech and clothing, stories of the different people who had come to the fortress, and why. There was nothing, however, that gave them the slightest clue as to how or why the Prince had ended up in Fred's bedroom.

By the time they'd been through it all, Fred and Rebecca were sick from the lingering smell and tired from leafing through the stacks of paper. Fred's dad had phoned to say he'd been delayed at the office but would be home shortly. The Prince himself reappeared in the doorway of the living room.

"Since you so rudely disapprove of our methods of finding our way back to Tarn, we have come to see if you yourself have had better luck."

Fred looked up and sighed. "No," he replied.

The Prince looked very superior. "We thought not," he said. "It is a wizard that is needed here, not some commoners rustling through a bunch of papers."

"He really is a self-satisfied little twerp, isn't he," said Rebecca as they watched him pad softly back down the hall.

Fred's anger, however, had passed. Something less certain had replaced it and Fred could not bring himself to answer.

Chapter Nine

𝒯he Prince did not wake up and demand breakfast the next morning. He stayed in bed with his back towards the world and a pillow over his head. Fred knew he was sulking. It was exactly what Fred himself did when he wanted to sulk.

That was fine with Fred. Fred didn't want to think about the Prince. He wanted to watch Saturday morning cartoons and not think about anything at all. All the cartoons were reruns, but that was even better, as far as Fred was concerned. He didn't have to think and he didn't have to pay attention, either. Maybe gnomelings were smarter than the Prince gave them credit for.

After a while Fred heard his dad shuffle into the kitchen and begin cracking eggs for their usual weekend breakfast of French toast. He went in to help him.

Fred's dad was doing exactly what he did every Saturday morning, but he didn't look the same as he usually did.

Instead of being dressed, he was standing at the kitchen counter in his housecoat and slippers. His hair was tousled and his eyes sleepy as he beat the eggs and milk and warmed the frying pan.

"Dad?" asked Fred. "Are you all right?"

His dad smiled. "Yes, Fred. I'm all right. I'm tired, that's all. The manuscript you showed me last night—I stayed up and read it."

"And?" asked Fred.

"It's a wonderful story. It's full of hope. It shows how much your mother, even when she was sick for so long, still believed in the goodness of life. I'd forgotten that. And I'd forgotten the importance of Tarn itself."

His dad reached up and brought down the muffin bowl. Fred understood then that they were also going to bake a peace offering for Mrs. Tobias to make up for last night's smoke bomb.

"Dad?"

"Yes?"

"I remembered some things about Mom last night too. I think..."

"What, Fred?" asked his dad gently.

"I think I've been missing her without even knowing it."

"Oh, Fred," said his dad.

"It all happened when I was really little," said Fred. "Shouldn't I be too old to miss her?"

"How could you be too old?" asked his dad. "You've never been nine, or ten, or eleven without a mom before."

"I never thought of it that way," said Fred.

"I should have realized," said his dad. "I'm sorry."

"It's not your fault," said Fred. "I can even handle it, missing her, I mean. I just wonder...do you think maybe that's why I feel so empty sometimes? Like nothing matters?"

His dad gave him a hug.

"*You* matter, Fred," said his dad. "That's what Tarn is all about."

"It is?" asked Fred.

"Yes," said his dad. "Mind you, like most stories, it's about a lot of other things too. But it takes time to figure it all out."

"You can say that again," said Fred.

By ten o'clock the French toast had been eaten and the muffins baked, but the Prince was still in bed. Fred's dad dressed and took some muffins over to Mrs. Tobias. While he was gone, Fred again checked his Prince of Tarn book.

The border was thicker now, and here and there trees had begun to infringe on the lettering itself. He closed the book quickly and pushed it extra deep beneath the cushions as he heard his father return.

"I'll never make sense of Mrs. Tobias if I live to be a hundred," said Fred's father. "Last night she was ranting and raving in the hallways about the smoke from our apartment. This morning she was nice as pie, thanked me very much for the muffins and insisted on filling up the plate with these awful little pink things she's always making us. You don't like them either, do you?"

Fred shook his head.

"I'll leave them here in the cupboard," said his father. "Maybe we can feed them to the Prince later. Is he awake yet?"

"He's sulking," said Fred.

"Well, at least he stays in character," said Fred's father. "But we better drag him out. I've got to go to work for a bit—you two can hang out on the office computers. After that we can pick up groceries."

"No, we'll find something to do here," said Fred. "But you go ahead. Make sure you get lots of food. Hisroy might be around for longer than we first thought."

Fred sat at the table for a long time after his father left. He sat staring at something in the sink. It was the tins the muffins had been baked in. They'd been washed, but they hadn't been put away. They were just sitting on the drain rack. The tea towel had been left in a lump on the counter. The jam jar had been left in the middle of the table. His father had left the kitchen clean, but in a friendly sort of way. It made Fred feel better. He decided there were things he, too, could do.

He stood up and went to the cupboard. He took down a recipe book and found a recipe for pizza dough. It wasn't easy. Even with the special new yeast his dad always bought he still had to knead all the ingredients and let the stuff rise. Slowly, however, he managed to make something that looked and acted like dough. He topped it with tinned tomato sauce and mushrooms. There was only a small bit of cheese, but he shredded it and figured it would do.

He cooked it, sliced it, put it on the silver tray they used at Christmas, and carried it in to the Prince.

"Good morning, Your Most Royal and Eminent Highness," said Fred.

The Prince didn't move.

"The Kitchens regret that they are unable to send strawberries, pheasant and isle cakes, but hope this Pizza will be to His Royal Highness's liking."

The Prince rolled over. His head was still beneath his pillow.

"After you have breakfasted, if His Royal Highness still wishes, we have jugglers to provide entertainment. They are performing in a park near here for His Highness's enjoyment."

The Prince lifted the pillow and opened one eye.

"We hope His Royal Highness enjoys his morning meal. We shall leave it here by the bed and shall return shortly with a finger bowl."

Fred set the tray down and left the room. He heard the bedsprings crunch behind him and knew the Prince was indeed sitting up to reach for a piece of pizza.

In the kitchen, Fred found an empty yogurt container that was deep enough so it wouldn't slosh when he carried it as a finger bowl. At least it was better than having to find bat dung, he thought as he filled it with water at the sink. And, with luck, there really would be jugglers in the park today, there often were on a Saturday.

After that—well, Fred just wasn't going to think about "after that." Today, at least, Fred would treat Hisroy as a prince.

And so began what Fred decided later was one of the best

days of his life. The truth was, the Prince was meant to be spoiled. He was written to be spoiled. It was like a game, and once Fred began to play it—really play it, in earnest—he and the Prince and everyone around them were pulled into a magic that was larger than life.

That afternoon in the park they were the Prince of Tarn and his Noble Servant Fred. They climbed trees where it was forbidden and—much to Fred's amazement and delight—everyone ignored them.

They waded in fountains where human feet were not allowed to tread, and passersby merely smiled.

They walked the high fence-rail without fear of falling. They rode the great marble lions at the gates. They slid down the stone cape on the statue of the city founder.

They picked great bouquets of flowers from the gardens, and wherever they picked one flower, two grew up in its place.

Little old men bought them kites to fly. Ice cream vendors pressed cones into their hands. Chipmunks sat on their shoulders. Small children laughed at them. Dogs played with them. Little old ladies fed them peppermints.

For one great and glorious afternoon, Fred knew what it was like to be spoiled—to be as completely and utterly spoiled as the Prince of Tarn.

And then, suddenly, the light of the day was mellowing. Fred and the Prince saw Rebecca coming across the park. They ran to greet her and walk home with her and tell her all the stories of the day.

"You got away with all that!" said Rebecca. "And ice cream

too? Nothing neat like that ever happens to me! I spent the whole afternoon being told what a mess I was making of the Minuet in G!"

Fred invited her for lemonade in the apartment—partly to make up for her missing out and partly because he wanted the day to never end. He served the lemonade in great tall glasses. And because they looked so beautiful, he took the plate of pink squares Mrs. Tobias had baked and set it on the table.

The Prince looked at the plate of squares and smiled hugely. He reached forward and took one. He opened his mouth and set it on his tongue. He closed his mouth, and a wonderfully dreamy expression passed over his features. His delight was so complete that Fred and Rebecca watched him happily. After a few moments, the square consumed, he opened his eyes.

"It is the perfect ending to a perfect day," announced the Prince. "Our only regret is that the plan has not worked."

"The plan?" asked Fred.

"What plan?" asked Rebecca.

"The plan to convince me to stay," said the Prince. "That was what you were up to, Fred, was it not?"

"Trying to make him stay?" asked Rebecca. "But Fred, you don't even like...That is, at first you couldn't stand..." She looked from Fred to the Prince and back again. "Of course that's what you were trying to do!"

"But I cannot stay," said the Prince decisively. "We are made for Tarn and Tarn is made for us, no matter how wonderful your isle cakes."

"What?" asked Fred.

"We *are* Tarn. It is in our blood and our..."

"No, no," said Fred. "What did you say about isle cakes?"

The Prince gestured to the plate of pink squares on the table. "They are every bit as good as those made by Rida, the castle's head cook, but still I cannot..."

"These are isle cakes?" asked Fred.

"Yes. Did you not know that? Did you not make them for me?"

"I didn't make them at all," said Fred. "I've never even heard of them until you showed up. I thought they were something just from Tarn."

The Prince looked at Rebecca.

"Did you make them?" he asked.

She shook her head.

"Then who?" asked the Prince.

"The lady who lives next door, Mrs. Tobias, sent them over," said Fred.

"The lady next door! With the orange hair? And the feet that flap? Who always wants to cut my hair?"

Fred and Rebecca nodded.

The Prince grinned widely.

"You never know what shape a wizard might take," he said.

He leapt out of his chair and headed for the door.

"Wait!" said Fred. "Wait! There's things you don't know! Hisroy!"

But the door was open and the Prince was through and all Fred could do was follow.

Chapter Ten

$\mathcal{M}$rs. Tobias was holding a pair of scissors when she opened the door.

"Have you come for a haircut?" she asked.

"No indeed," said the Prince.

The Prince looked princely and waltzed on into the apartment. Rebecca followed him. That left Fred standing at the door with Mrs. Tobias, wondering what he should say.

"Actually," said Fred, "actually...er...we've come to...er...to thank you for the isle cakes. They were delicious."

"They were?" asked Mrs. Tobias.

"Yes," said Fred.

A smile spread over Mrs. Tobias's face. It spread slowly, but it was a true smile. In fact, she practically beamed.

"Why, thank you, Fred," she said. "All these years I've been making them and that's the first time you've come to say thank you."

She looked over her shoulder and her usual worried expression took over again.

"What are they doing? I don't much like them wandering round my living room."

"I know. I'm sorry. It's just..." He leaned forward to whisper to Mrs. Tobias. He wasn't at all sure he wanted the Prince to hear. "Mrs. Tobias, about the isle cakes, where did you get the recipe?"

"Why, from your mother, of course," said Mrs. Tobias. "That's why I always send them over to you."

Fred felt a great rush of relief. Neighbours exchanged recipes all the time. It didn't mean Mrs. Tobias knew any more than that. Mrs. Tobias looked over her shoulder again.

"I think I'd better keep an eye on them," she said, turning back to the apartment.

Fred followed her through the door. Even though they had lived beside each other for years and years, he had never been in Mrs. Tobias's apartment. In layout, of course, it was very much like his own, but there the similarities ended. Fred's apartment was spare and uncluttered. In Mrs. Tobias's apartment every wall, every floor space, every counter or cabinet was covered by a craft item of some sort. Needlework, popsicle-stick art, knitting, crocheting, leather work, silk flowers, dried flowers, bottle-cap art, dough art, bead work, art from feathers, plastic and egg cartons, and more—it was all there in surprising shapes and varieties and uses.

The Prince was wandering the rooms looking at everything, with Rebecca following close behind him. Even

Fred, who knew it wasn't really polite, couldn't help gawking a bit.

"A very interesting dren," announced the Prince. "Do you have any owls?"

Mrs. Tobias pointed to the top of her kitchen shelves. There, peering down, was a row of owls. Ceramic owls, wooden owls, owls made of pom poms and papier mâché and seashells.

"Very wise of you," said the Prince. "Live owls are nothing but trouble."

"Fred," said Rebecca softly. She was pointing towards a row of books on the kitchen counter. One of them had a brown leather binding the same as Fred's own *Prince of Tarn*.

"Time to go," said Fred.

"But Fred, the book! Don't you see it?" whispered Rebecca.

"Time to go," said Fred, firmly taking the Prince by the arm.

The Prince was not about to leave. He looked at Fred and looked at Rebecca and then looked at the books on the counter.

"Madam," said the Prince to Mrs. Tobias, "in which of these books are the magic spells?"

"Magic spells?" asked Mrs. Tobias. "Well, yes, there are all sorts of very strange things written in that book, but Fred's mother gave it to me and I treasure it. I wouldn't want anyone to take it away."

"We only wish to see," said the Prince, "which one would it be."

He reached forward but Fred was too quick for him. He put out a hand and snatched the leather-bound book.

"It is my book, Fred," said Mrs. Tobias. "You can see that your mother wrote in it when she gave it to me."

Fred opened the cover. Inside was written, "To my dearest neighbour and friend, Annabella Marie Tobias, with enormous amounts of love."

There then followed a signature which was his mother's name but, Fred realized as he looked at it, was not her handwriting. For that matter, the inscription itself wasn't done in his mother's handwriting either. Fred glanced up at Mrs. Tobias, but did not say anything.

"We wish to see," said the Prince.

Fred handed the book quickly to Rebecca. He figured Rebecca, being bossier, would be able to hold onto it better than he could. As he handed it across, a page slipped out. The Prince caught it as it fell, glanced at it and began to read aloud.

"The Great Hall of Tarn forms the centre of the fortress. It is made of marble and inlaid with..." He looked up. "Clearly written by someone who has visited Tarn," he said.

"Yes, it mentions Tarn all the time," said Mrs. Tobias. "Is that what you children are doing? Playing some sort of imaginary game about Tarn? I don't mind you checking the rules, but you're not to take it away. That book was given to me and..."

The Prince, who had been reading silently, now interrupted with a sniff of disdain.

"Well, the bit about the fortress itself isn't too bad, but

they could have at least been accurate about the rest of Tarn," he said. "It says the fortress is surrounded by villages and farmlands. That's a lot of rot. The forests are so thick and overgrown no one hunts beyond the river, let alone lives there. And this bit about travellers on the roads between Tindlegate and Tarn, or Tarn and the Southlands. What a fairy tale! No one goes beyond the castle walls on the east and the river on the west."

"Because of the forests?" asked Fred.

"Of course because of the forests! I just told you that! They're quite impenetrable."

"But when you arrived in my bedroom you were calling for the Stable Master, horses and food for travelling," said Fred.

"A prince has to say something. People EXPECT something from a prince."

"How long has it been like that?" asked Fred.

"The forests?" asked the Prince. "They've been like that forever. Or at least as long as I remember. I think. Ezran plays around with time. I've told you that. It makes it hard to sort things out sometimes."

"It is a hard book to sort out," said Mrs. Tobias. "Although I've managed to use it for several things, if I do say so myself."

The Prince was reading the back of the page.

"And listen to this! It talks about Ezran—youthful and vibrant wizard of the twelfth level! Hah! Ezran's as old and bent as an apple tree."

"Are you sure?" asked Fred. "I never thought of Ezran as being that old."

"I really don't understand how you know so much about some things and so little about everything else," said the Prince, shaking his head impatiently. "Ezran wasn't old, not at first. But lately Ezran's gotten old faster than everyone else. At least it seems like it's faster. I don't know! Wizards are wizards and there are things princes simply are not told!"

Fred leaned across to read over the Prince's shoulder. Although part of him wanted to get the Prince as far away from all this as possible, especially after what he'd said about the forests and about Ezran, another part of him couldn't help but want to see.

"'Ezran the wizard is master of the secrets of healing, familiar of animals, keeper of the sacred texts and all manner of spells,'" read Fred. "'Ezran has been charged by Elisia and Ferin with the Protection of all of Tarn, and above all with the protection of the Prince himself.'"

"Someone should read that to Ezran," said the Prince.

"Maybe you'll be able to read it to Ezran yourself," said Rebecca.

Fred and the Prince turned to her. While the Prince had been reading the sheet of loose paper, Rebecca had been leafing through the book itself.

"You've found something!" said the Prince.

"Rebecca," cautioned Fred.

But Rebecca was too excited to hear and frankly, Fred knew, there was no way to stop things now.

"It's like Mrs. Tobias said," said Rebecca. "It's a book with all sorts of things in it—a kind of registry. In the front are the names and birth dates of all the main characters."

"Main characters of what?" asked the Prince.

"She means the main residents of Tarn," said Fred.

"Right," said Rebecca. "And in the middle are recipes and poems and words of wisdom, Tarn-style—well, like the one Mrs. Tobias has on her wall in the living room."

"'Giants are conquered, not in spite of their size, but because of it,'" recited Mrs. Tobias from memory. "Done in counted cross-stitch."

"And in the back are the magic spells of Ezran the wizard," said Rebecca.

"Indeed!" cried the Prince.

He reached for the book, but Rebecca was truthfully very good at holding onto things.

"There's quite a few of them," said Rebecca. "Let's see... there's the spell for turning young princes into frogs."

"Stay away from that one," said the Prince. "It's not at all pleasant."

"There's a spell for the gift of flight," continued Rebecca.

"Ezran told me it was impossible! I've asked and asked for ever so long to be allowed to fly and Ezran said it couldn't be done!"

"And a spell for changing form," said Rebecca.

"I KNOW Ezran does that," said the Prince resignedly. "When you least expect someone, there's Ezran. And besides, it has side effects. The time Ezran was a garden statue there was clay falling from the Royal Wizard's robe for at least a week. Most unpleasant."

"The side effects for the next one don't sound too lovely either," said Rebecca. "Something about the weight of time itself coming to bear on the shoulders of those who try to hold it back."

"I can't help it if Ezran chooses to do things with time. I've told you that. It's not what we're looking for!" said the Prince. "It's travel spells we need."

"And there are several spells for the transportation of bodies," said Rebecca.

The Prince jumped up. "That's it. That's the one we want. What does it say?"

"Just a minute," said Rebecca. "I have to turn the page."

Both Fred and the Prince watched her. Mrs. Tobias watched too, but she seemed concerned only with how carefully the page was turned, not with what was written upon it.

"Spell number one," read Rebecca. "'...the words of the Exanar, repeated forwards, backwards and then forwards again, ending the final time with the names of both the traveller and the destination.'"

The Prince scowled. "That's no help whatsoever. The Exanar is written in a language no one but Ezran can even pronounce, let alone remember. I think Ezran made it up."

"Spell number two," read Rebecca. "'The words of the Ezubial, repeated with...'"

"The Ezubial! Even worse!" interrupted the Prince.

"And last of all," said Rebecca, with a smile and a pause. "Spell number three. 'Homecoming spell, transporting the traveller and all beneath his or her hand to the traveller's own true home. The single spell-word "Eltadore" when pronounced by the traveller upon the sacred mark of the traveller's birth.'"

Rebecca and Fred both looked at the Prince. Rebecca looked with expectation and Fred looked with fear. Instead of being overjoyed at this discovery, however, the Prince was totally devastated.

"Hopeless," he said. "Not only hopeless, but totally foolish at that."

"All you have to do is remember one word!" said Rebecca.

"It's not the word, it's the other part of it. The sacred mark of my birth exists in only one place—the centre of the Great Hall of Tarn. And if I were standing there, I would already be home. I should think that would be obvious to anyone, even a commoner." He turned to Mrs. Tobias. "Madam—are you or are you not a wizard?"

"Me?" asked Mrs. Tobias. A funny little smile and a red flush crept slowly to her features. She was, Fred realized, oddly flattered. "Well...I...I'm very talented at many things and yes, thank you, I do certainly pride myself on being a bit out of the ordinary. A bit mysterious even, perhaps. But no, I wouldn't say I'm a wizard."

"And have you no way at all of returning me to my home?"

"I don't even drive a car, I'm afraid," said Mrs. Tobias apologetically.

"Then I must thank you for your kindness and hospitality and be gone," said the Prince.

He spun around on his heel and left the apartment.

Chapter Eleven

When Fred and Rebecca returned to Fred's apartment a few minutes later, they found Fred's father standing in the kitchen in the midst of several bags of half-unpacked groceries.

"The Prince just came through here," he said. "He informed me that the lady with the flapping feet is not a wizard and went down to the bedroom and closed the door. I take it I've missed something."

"Hisroy got excited because those little pink things Mrs. Tobias bakes are a lot like the isle cakes he's always asking for—but all she had was an old recipe," said Fred. "No big deal."

Rebecca opened her mouth to protest. Fred gave a short sharp shake of his head. Together they went out on the balcony. Fred figured no one but the birds could hear them out there.

"No big deal!" said Rebecca. "Fred, that little book's important. I know it is! I don't know why your mom gave it to Mrs. Tobias but..."

"Mom didn't give it to her," said Fred. "Mrs. Tobias wrote the inscription in it herself. Either she stole it or maybe it fell in with other things by accident and Mrs. Tobias found it when she was poking around in the garbage looking for stuff for her projects. Anyway, it doesn't matter."

"Of course it matters!" said Rebecca. "Fred, there must be some way to make those magic spells work."

"You're forgetting what the Prince said about the forests," said Fred.

"The forests?" asked Rebecca.

Fred was looking at her hard.

"Well, okay, let me think," she said. "He said something about there being forests all grown up around some places."

"Not just some places," said Fred. "Everywhere. Everything being taken back by..."

"Trees," said Rebecca. "Oh, Fred, the trees."

Fred went into the living room and brought the book out to her. Trees rolled, thick and heavy, across the pages now, in places totally obscuring whole sections of writing.

"I don't understand," said Rebecca. "This isn't happening in the typewritten manuscript, or the notebooks, or even the book Mrs. Tobias has."

"Those aren't the same. They're part of it, they set everything up, but the Prince's story is here, on these pages. The world he lives in is on these pages."

Rebecca looked up at Fred. "The trees aren't just taking over in the book," she said. "Is that what you're saying? They're taking over in Tarn as well?"

"Maybe not taking over, exactly. It's more as if everything is falling back. The story grew out of my mom's imagination—the doodling, the trees. It became more than just imagination because of what my dad said about how she was different when she wrote..."

"The smells and sounds and smoke under the door," said Rebecca.

"Exactly," said Fred. "And it was so good and so detailed that even after she finished working on it, it was still there. At first." Fred looked across at the hills beyond the city. "Then it began to fall back to imagination again, back to the trees, just like in the book," he said.

"But it couldn't have happened as fast as it is here and now, on these pages," said Rebecca. "There wouldn't be anything left."

Fred nodded his agreement. He didn't know for certain, of course, but he could guess what it would have been like.

"It must have begun very slowly, with just a few new and mysterious trees on the outermost edge of Tarn. People wouldn't have realized what was happening, just as we didn't understand it in the book, at first. Then later, when some of them did begin to realize, what could they do about it? Ferin and Elisia tried visiting the outlying areas and never returned to the castle. Ezran must have tried all sorts of magic. And finally, perhaps when the trees were within sight of the castle walls themselves, Ezran must have tried to slow the flow of time itself. As old and bent as an apple tree—isn't that how Hisroy described Ezran? The weight of time itself on the shoulders of those who try to hold it back, just like in the spell."

Rebecca nodded.

"But apparently even a wizard cannot stop time entirely," said Fred. "The magic is wearing out."

"Then Ezran sent him here, not as punishment, but to save him," said Rebecca.

"I think so," said Fred. "I don't want my dad to know yet. Tarn matters to my dad in some way I don't understand."

"Maybe we're both getting carried away," said Rebecca. "Maybe the trees don't mean anything at all."

"Maybe," said Fred.

But he could tell by the look on Rebecca's face that she didn't believe it either.

It was late when Fred and his father finished eating that night. Rebecca had gone home. The Prince had not come out of Fred's room for supper. Fred went through the box with the manuscript and notebooks one last time. He wasn't reading them, exactly, just sorting through them, looking at them. He even made a few lines on the bottom of one page with the plastic pen from the box. The lines came out in the same blue-black ink in which all the notebooks were written. He couldn't think of anything else he could look for.

At ten o'clock Mrs. Tobias rapped on the wall (Fred was allowed an extra hour on weekends).

"I think the Prince has pulled the dresser across the door to bar it," said Fred's father. "Maybe he's really going back this time. I know you're getting to like him, Fred, but it's better if he's back where he belongs. Do you think you could sleep in the living room?"

"Sure," said Fred. He fetched some blankets and a spare pillow from the hall closet and settled down on the sofa.

"Is something wrong, Fred?" asked his father, looking down at him. "I'm glad we talked about what we did this morning, but if there's something else..."

"No," said Fred quickly. "It's all right."

But of course it wasn't all right. How could he tell his dad that even the brightest sparks of imagination do not last forever?

"Fred?"

It was morning, and someone was standing in the middle of the living room. For a moment, in that strange haze between wakefulness and sleeping, Fred thought it was himself.

"Fred, I've come to say goodbye."

It was the Prince, of course. Just at that moment, the first rays of the sun broke over the hills. As Fred watched through sleep-thick eyes, Hisroy turned to face the light streaming through the glass doors. He was dressed as when he had first arrived in Fred's room, in tunic and tights, and he carried a rolled bundle that looked like a couple of bath towels or something under one arm.

Fred struggled to prop himself up on his elbow.

"What do you mean, goodbye?" asked Fred.

"I am returning to Tarn," said the Prince. "I understand now that there will be no easy way. It will be a journey and a quest and I shall have to prove myself up to it. I am setting out on foot this morning."

"You mean you're walking!" said Fred.

"I wish you to thank your father for his hospitality," said Hisroy with a nod of his head. "I wish to thank you, also, Fred. And Rebecca. I have borrowed a few things I feel I might need for the journey—some rations, a change of footwear, the bedroll. I bid you adieu."

He bowed in a grave and serious manner and walked to the door.

Fred rolled off the couch and scrambled after him. "Wait! You can't just go walking home."

"I must," said the Prince. "I can find no other way."

"But...But you won't know which way to go!" said Fred.

"I am the Prince of Tarn. I shall be guided. It will be part of what lies before me."

"But it's probably thousands of miles. Millions of miles!"

"I shall find my way. In time."

"You'll starve! You'll be mugged! You'll...you'll be run over by a bus!"

Fred could see his words were making no impression whatsoever. Whether it was a trick to get Ezran's attention, or some true crazy plan in the Prince's head, Fred didn't know. At this exact moment, however, the Prince seemed determined to carry it through. He opened the door and stepped out into the hall. Fred didn't have time to do anything but blurt it out.

"You can't go. There isn't a place called Tarn. It doesn't exist."

The Prince turned.

"I beg your pardon?"

"It doesn't exist," said Fred. "Tarn doesn't exist. It's a story. Out of a book."

The Prince looked hard at Fred.

"I am disappointed in you, Fred. I had thought at this moment of parting you would, at least, rise above yourself. I did not expect jokes."

"It's not a joke. It's true," said Fred.

He was scrambling again, this time across the living room.

"Tarn's a book. It's all from a book. This book."

He held it up. He hurried forward and put it in the Prince's hands.

"Open it," said Fred. "It's about you. You're a character from a book. My mom wrote it. She wrote lots of books. And lots of characters. She just...wrote you better than most."

The Prince held the book by the very tips of his fingers as if it was a trick box. Or a mousetrap.

"Open it," said Fred.

Still the Prince eyed Fred suspiciously. Fred nodded. The Prince looked down at the small book in his hands. He looked at Fred. He looked down and, very slowly, opened the book. He looked at the first page. And then the second. And then the third and fourth and fifth. He closed the book. He handed it back to Fred. The look on his face was one of pity.

"It is a book of trees," said the Prince. "I am sorry that my leaving drives you to such desperate lengths, but leave I must. It is time. I feel it."

Fred opened the book. No printing at all remained. All was forests, wonderful forests dark and tangled—imagination, but imagination without form.

"No. Wait!" cried Fred, for the Prince was now in the corridor. "That's the whole problem. The trees! Hisroy—I wouldn't lie to you. I'm your friend!"

Again the Prince turned.

"Tarn doesn't exist," pleaded Fred. "It's just a place in a book. And you're a character. From a book."

"I am not a character from a book!" said the Prince. "If anyone is from a book it's you—you and your strange way of living piled one on the other, and your strange ways of travelling in machines that gobble you, and your gnomeling ways of entertaining yourselves, and your complete lack of magic. If anything is a story, you are! And a preposterous one! And I am about to find my way out of it!"

At that moment the stairwell door at the end of the hall opened. Rebecca came running towards them.

"Fred! I had to come! I couldn't sleep all night, so I finally woke up my mom and told her about everything. Tindlegate and Southlands, Fred—Mom says they're real places. That is, they're not real, real—but they stand for places that were real. Your mom and dad's homes, Fred. Both your mom and dad come from homes where there was a lot of fighting and a lot of unhappiness. That's why your dad won't ever talk about his family, or your mom's relations either. That's why Tarn is so important to him. Tarn is the safe place, the good place your mom and dad wanted to make for themselves. And for you. You're the Prince of Tarn, Fred. I mean, Hisroy's the Prince, but you are too, in a way. Mom said she'll try and help us and..."

She looked at Fred and the Prince and the bundle under his arm.

"What's going on?" she asked.

"I am going home," said the Prince.

"He thinks he can walk his way back to Tarn," said Fred.

"Tell him about the book!" said Rebecca. "Show him the book!"

"I have," said Fred. "He doesn't believe me."

"He has to believe you," said Rebecca. She turned to the Prince. "You can't go."

"I must," said the Prince. "And I don't want to hear any more about stories or characters or..."

He turned to walk away. Rebecca grabbed at his arm, but got his bundle instead. The Prince tried to yank it from her. Rebecca yanked back. Fred could see the Prince setting his muscles. He reached out and grabbed his own corner of the bundle to give Rebecca a hand. As his hands went around it he realized it wasn't a couple of bath towels at all, it was the old quilt from his bedroom, and he almost let go for fear of ripping it.

But at that moment the Prince pulled.

And Rebecca pulled.

And Fred couldn't help but pull.

There was indeed a great ripping noise, not the noise of the quilt itself being torn in two, but the tearing of the patches that had been used to cover it.

Fred found himself with a piece of red material in his hands. Rebecca found herself with a piece of blue stripes. The Prince was fallen back on the floor. Across him, with a few escaped belongings, lay the quilt itself. It was the quilt the way it had been originally sewn, with scraps of the pattern worn and missing but the design recognizable still. Rebecca and Fred stared at it and stared at it.

There was no mistake. The pattern on the quilt was the wonderful eagle of Tarn.

"Like the one etched in marble on the floor of the Great Hall," said Fred.

"Surrounded by three circles and holding a golden stick, exactly as the story describes it," said Rebecca. "The sacred mark of birth!"

The Prince looked at Rebecca and then at Fred and then at the quilt as it lay upon him. He leapt to his feet.

"A story!" he cried with a triumphant laugh. "A story indeed! We shall show you how much of a story!"

He touched the quilt to his lips, as travellers in olden days are said to have kissed the earth itself, and dropped it with a flourish to his feet. With one hand on Fred's shoulder and another on Rebecca's arm, before either of them could think fast enough to truly understand what he was doing, he spoke the single spell-word while standing on the sacred mark of his birth.

"Eltadore."

And although it might be expected that Mrs. Tobias would appear in the hallway at any time during all the yelling and fighting to find out what was going on, in fact she did not. She had misplaced her teeth that morning. She did not like to appear without them. It was only during the last moments of the argument that she found her teeth and snapped them in place and went to open the door.

By then Fred, Rebecca and the Prince had disappeared. All she found was an old quilt spread on the hallway floor and a scrap of red material spiralling slowly down to meet it—like a kite just released from the tail end of a wind.

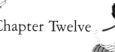

Chapter Twelve

"What's happening?"

Fred wasn't sure if it was his cry or Rebecca's. They were caught in a great, swirling wind. It whipped closer and closer around them and rose, rose—except *they* did not rise. They did not spin. They were the quiet centre. All around was tumult and light, but they seemed to grow quieter and quieter.

And now the little quiet space that was the three of them began to be somehow stronger than what was without. It seemed to be pushing back the tumult, quieting the wind. And finally all was still and they were looking up into the high, high arches of a hall, a great hall, all over and around them. Sunlight streamed down in broad rich bands and all was light and air.

"The Great Hall of Tarn," whispered Fred.

"Now you shall see!" said the Prince. "Book, indeed!"

And he strode out across the great marble floor calling, "Guards! Guards!" in a grand voice.

"Maybe we should have been a whole lot nicer to him," said Rebecca, her eyes fixed on the Prince.

"I don't understand," said Fred. "I don't understand why it's still here. But look at it, Rebecca. It's even more real, more wonderful than I've ever imagined."

The Great Hall was indeed magnificent. The windows were intricacies of multi-coloured glass. The stonework was etched with delicate patterns. There were wonderful murals of inlaid black and white stone. Had all this come from his mother's imagination? Had she truly seen it all as richly as this? Or would even she have been amazed?

Fred then noticed a tree growing in the corner of the Great Hall. It was just a small tree, maybe a foot taller than Fred, but a tree nevertheless. Fred walked over to it. Its roots seemed fixed in the stone itself.

Meanwhile the Prince was pacing back and forth calling, "Guards!" but there was no answer.

"They've grown incredibly lax while I've..." the Prince paused and gave a small smug smile before correcting himself, "while *we've* been gone. We'll soon fix that."

He strode out of the room. Fred and Rebecca followed him. They entered a wide passage, where two trees stood tall and straight by the door, and turned right. The hallway skirted the outside of the Great Hall and then led along in another direction. It too was empty, but here and there, in ones and twos, trees stood.

110

At first the Prince merely strode past the trees, ignoring them. Gradually, however, his pace began to falter as he approached yet another, and another. He began to look at them out of the corner of his eye. By one tall window, where three trees stood around a small table, he stopped and looked at them directly.

Still he did not look at Fred or Rebecca but turned towards a staircase. Up he climbed, taking the steps three at a time, until he came to a heavy wooden door. Without knocking, the Prince pushed through the door and burst into the room with the protest, "Ezran, this really is too much. The whole castle is overgrown with..."

And there he stopped, for the room was empty, empty except for the paraphernalia of wizards—rows of beakers and flasks, jars and powders and cobwebs and—a tree. A knobby, gnarly tree in the middle of the room, with its limbs outstretched, reaching heavenward, pleading, despairing, perhaps even trying to cast one last spell to save them all. It was a tree of such ugliness that at first Fred didn't want to look at it.

Look he must, however, for he was convinced, as he knew Rebecca was convinced beside him, that this gnarled and time-scarred tree was Ezran.

The Prince was staring as well. Staring and staring. With one hand he reached out to touch the bark, the twisted, knotty limbs, the tip of one twig.

He pulled his hand back and looked sharply around the room. There were several small trees growing in the dren as well. One was perched atop a shelf. Another sat fixed to a cuckoo clock. A third was straining into the air from the loft railing above them as if attempting flight.

"The owls," whispered Rebecca. "Even the owls."

For several long minutes the Prince stood there looking. At last he drew himself up tall.

"We shall withdraw to the throne," he announced. Turning, he left the room.

This time the Prince walked slowly and solemnly through the castle. Fred and Rebecca followed him at a distance. They couldn't help peering in doorways. In one room six looms were set up, six looms tended by six young ash trees. In another room a beautiful willow was lovingly curled around the strings of a harp. In what must have been the royal accounting chamber, trees grew in and among the desks and ink wells. In another room a lesson was being taught by an oak tree to nine saplings—two birch, two poplar, four spruce and a tamarack. And in the kitchens two mountain ash shaded a cutting board while a small, aged apple tree tended a pot of stew in the hearth.

Fred slipped across the kitchen and peered into the pot. He touched the side with his fingers.

"How long ago?" asked Rebecca.

"It's cold, but it doesn't smell bad or anything," said Fred.

"This morning, then," said Rebecca. "Or yesterday."

"Yesterday, I think," said Fred.

"Would it have happened all at once? All of them all at once?" asked Rebecca.

"More or less, I think. And from the roots up," said Fred.

The roots and trunks of the trees seemed very tree-like, but the upper limbs retained the merest hint of human form. "It's as if they didn't know it was happening, somehow, or at least were resigned to it. They seem to have been just going about their daily jobs and at the same time slowly turning into trees."

"Except for Ezran," said Rebecca. "Ezran was fighting it."

Fred nodded.

They hurried to follow the Prince. At the entranceway to the Great Hall he stopped before one of the two trees guarding the doorway. It was tall and lean and seemed to have a special air about it. The Prince's face was white and strained as he looked up at it.

"Garrick, special bodyguard to the Prince of Tarn," said the Prince. He looked at Fred and Rebecca, and then back at Garrick. "I spent many hours hiding from him. He spent many hours finding me. We both became very, very good at it."

The Prince walked into the Great Hall and up to the small tree they had first seen.

"Cira, a serving girl," he told Fred and Rebecca. "And one of the very best at playing Snake by Twos."

He walked across the hall to the throne and sat down.

"I think you're being very brave," said Rebecca.

"You think I'm a 'self-satisfied little twerp,'" said the Prince.

"That was different," said Rebecca.

But the Prince raised a regal hand. "And a self-satisfied little twerp is what I am. How could I not have known something was going wrong? How could I have thought Ezran sent me away because of some silly mice, or as part of my education or for a party? A party!"

"They didn't want you to know," said Rebecca. "They sent you away so you wouldn't know, wouldn't be part of it."

"I should have figured it out! I am the Prince. Tarn is what I am and why I am!" He stood and walked to the door and back again—bewildered and angry and frustrated with being unable to understand. "Why has this happened?" he demanded of the air around him.

"It's because all this," said Fred quietly, "is a story from a book."

The Prince sank with peculiar helplessness onto the throne. "Tell me," he said.

Fred sat on the dais of the throne and told things as best he could. He told about his mother's doodling and her imagination and the trees. He told about the manuscript and the notebooks. He told what his dad had said about her needing so badly to believe in the goodness of life. And then, because the Prince asked to hear it, with Rebecca's help he told the story of Tarn itself and how it had come to be.

It was late in Tarn when Fred finished his story. Fred was not sure of the passage of time at home, but here the sun was already slanting low through the side windows. The Prince, who had listened silently, only now and then asking a question, remained seated on the throne.

"Then I have lasted longest, it seems, because I was the most detailed of all her characters."

"And the one she loved the most," said Rebecca.

"But if you do not come back with us, even you will not last forever," said Fred.

The Prince smiled sadly and shook his head.

"I will not come back with you," he said. "Tarn is my home. Ezran, and the others, all the others upon whom I play tricks—and am tricked upon in turn—are part of me." The Prince stood. "It grows dark. The castle becomes chill at night."

He led them through the empty halls to a large room of cushions and lounges. In a room beyond that was a great canopied bed from which the Prince took rich throws, dividing them among the three of them. They were soft and long and welcome, for the cold was indeed creeping along the stones of the castle.

Fred and Rebecca made themselves beds among the cushions. The Prince wrapped himself in a throw and settled on the window seat, looking out into a courtyard increasingly dark and leafy.

Perhaps it was the early hour at which he had been woken, or perhaps it was the darkness itself, but Fred felt a great weariness come over him. It was a long time, however, before he actually felt sleep closing in, and even as he did he knew that the Prince was still awake, still awake and thinking in the night.

Chapter Thirteen

$\mathcal{M}$orning.

The sun streamed in from the courtyard, bringing light and lifting the chill. It fell across the rich pillows and throws, and touched the two young bodies that lay there.

Rebecca was already awake and looking at Fred. As if feeling her gaze upon him, Fred also opened his eyes. He looked for the Prince, did not see him, and sat up quickly.

"He said he was going to find us some breakfast," said Rebecca. "But I need to talk to you before he comes back. I've been thinking about how we'll get home, Fred."

"We'll use the spell," said Fred, "the one that brought us."

Rebecca was shaking her head.

"It only works for someone standing on the mark of their birth," she said. "Unless you have a secret family crest with an eagle on it or maybe were born on the quilt or something, it's not going to work for you or me, or even for the Prince, because he's already home."

Fred hadn't thought of that. "I don't know then," he said truthfully.

"The way I see it is this," said Rebecca. "Your mom took something from real life—the old quilt with the eagle on it—and used it as a symbol in Tarn. Right?"

Fred nodded.

"Then maybe she did it the other way around too. Maybe there is something in Tarn that is a symbol of your life. Your birth. But we have to find it. And we'd better start looking right away, because it seems to me there's ivy creeping up over the arches that wasn't here yesterday. And when we find something to take us home we'll have to trick the Prince in order to get him to come back with us."

Even as she spoke, Fred was pushing away the last threads of sleep and getting to his feet. Stepping between the robes and pillows, he made his way into the outer room and on to the hallway. There he stopped. A sense of helplessness fell heavily upon his shoulders.

The hallway and interconnecting passages seemed to go on forever. They'd be lucky if they could just keep from getting lost, let alone find what they were looking for. And already there were vines, not only twining over the archways, but threading across the stone floor as well.

"Maybe we should start at the Great Hall and work outward," said Rebecca, coming up behind him. She too must have felt the enormousness of their task, for her voice had lost some of its confidence. "I think it's this way."

Even knowing the general direction, it still took them several twists and turns and a doubling back before they found the great room that formed the heart of the castle. Nothing along the way seemed to Fred to be significant in his own life—no symbols, no signs. The Great Hall itself felt like an old friend, but Fred was pretty sure that was only because he was glad they really were able to find it again.

It was there that the Prince caught up with them.

"Good morning," he said, striding towards them with a tray which he set on the dais of the throne. "I was able to find some not-too-stale pastries in the kitchens. The cook is an apple tree, I think. She even looks as though she might blossom."

He said the words lightly, as if they meant nothing at all to him, but on the word blossom his voice cracked just for a moment. Nevertheless he carried on, handing out sweet breads and drinks smelling of spices in tall, glass mugs.

"They're hot!" said Rebecca.

"I didn't dare try the main hearth, with cook standing so close, but I was able to stir up a few embers at the back of the baker's oven," said the Prince.

There was something different about the Prince this morning, something that had started last night and grown stronger. 'I', Fred realized. The Prince was referring to himself as 'I' and not 'we', even here in Tarn.

Fred bit into the first pastry and realized he was indeed very hungry. The food and warm drinks seemed to make them all feel better. That was another thing different about the Prince.

He was the one serving breakfast!

"I discovered something else in the kitchen," said the Prince. "A leaf fell from the baker's branch when I knocked against him, and turned into a bit of piecrust. It has made me wonder..."

He stood and crossed the hall to the tree that was Garrick. He reached out and took hold of a knob of wood on the trunk of the tree. Rebecca sat up in alarm.

"No!" she cried.

There was a snapping sound. Fred and Rebecca looked at the Prince in horror. He walked to them and opened his hand. There in the palm lay a button.

"I know him so well, you see," said the Prince. "I could see him standing there within the tree. It was a bit of a chance to take, but Garrick would have understood. I am sure of it now: I shall be able to send you home."

"With a button?" asked Rebecca.

"With Ezran's staff. It has been turned to tree in Ezran's hand. The button, and Garrick, have proven that we can free it."

"Will it work for us? Don't we need Ezran or magic words or something?" asked Rebecca.

The Prince turned to Fred for an answer. Yes, Fred realized, the Prince was different this morning. He had grown less rude and less self-centred and all of this had made him more princely in other ways.

"Hisroy's used the staff before," Fred explained to Rebecca. "He sent the owls to the country of the giants. They were mad at him for weeks. And once he sent Garrick..."

Fred's words faded away. The Prince had raised his arm to drink the last of his hot drink, and a tiny tendril with a single leaf at the end had slipped from the cuff of his tunic. Rebecca had seen it too.

The Prince lowered his arm and tucked the leaf back in.

"You must come back with us," said Rebecca.

"Even if I were to agree, which I would not, it is already too late, I think," said the Prince. "Do not look so sad. It does not hurt. If I am, as you said yesterday, merely a storybook character, then it is not sad. All this is but a story, a dream. It is only imagination to which I return, nothing worse."

The words, Fred knew, were meant to make them feel better. It wasn't working. With every word he spoke the Prince was behaving less and less like a storybook character and more and more like a real prince.

"It does mean, however, that we should hurry. For your sakes," he said.

Fred and Rebecca downed the last of their own hot drinks and rose.

"This way is quickest," said the Prince, leading them towards the back of the room.

They climbed a small staircase. Instead of using the door at the top, however, the Prince pushed open one of three small windows and climbed through. A tendril from his heel caught on the sill as he passed over it. Rebecca lifted it quickly and followed.

They came out at a stone parapet within the castle walls. Again they climbed, leaping onto the wooden boards of a rooftop, crossing it, walking along a parapet again and jumping to another roof. From here they could see beyond the castle walls to the countryside. At one time, Fred knew, they would have been able to see roads and parklands, the roofs of village houses, bits of gardens, farmlands and fields. Now it was all trees as far as the eye could see.

The Prince did not pause to look. Perhaps he did not want to see. Perhaps it was hard enough for him just to walk, for there was a stiffness in his movements, and now and then another tendril drifted down from one of his heels to try to catch on the rooftop.

They reached the back side of a tower with, again, a small window. It was shut, but the Prince had no problem opening it. The three of them climbed into what Fred recognized as the loft of Ezran's dren where one of the owls had been, and was still, trying to fly from the railing.

On one side was a bed. On the other side were several volumes of books bound in maroon with gold writing on the spines. They looked like the encyclopædia in Fred's classroom, only there were just three of them. The Prince paused before them.

"The sacred texts," he said. "I thought one day I might be allowed to read them. They are so valued by Tarn that in all of time remembered, Ezran alone has looked upon their pages."

The Prince put his hand out, paused, and slowly withdrew it.

"No, it would be unkind for me to do so now. Ezran cannot even turn me into so much as a turnip as punishment. And there is no time," said the Prince. "Come."

He walked to the railing and looked over at the tree that was Ezran below.

"Yes, the staff, I was sure Ezran was holding it."

"I think I see it too," said Fred. "I'll help you."

Together they went down to the dren. Looking at the tree in the middle of the room with its branches upraised, Fred felt he could indeed see the face and the arms and now the fingers that were wrapped around the staff. Very carefully he and Hisroy were able to pry the woody fingers free. As they did so, Fred could feel the stick changing in his hand, becoming slim, golden and almost alive.

"Grasp it tightly," said the Prince. "It is a staff with a mind of its own. I fear my hands are no longer nimble enough to hold it."

Fred held it tightly.

"It would be best used in the Great Hall," said the Prince. "It is too close here to its master. We have time if we hurry."

They climbed back to the loft. Rebecca had her back to them. She jumped as they came in, turned and backed up to the table.

The Prince climbed first out the window. He was trailing long vines behind him now. Fred untwined one from a leg of the bed and made to follow him. Rebecca called him back.

"I know, I know," said Fred. "We have to trick him somehow, take him back with us. But I don't know how we're going to do it."

"It's not that," said Rebecca. She brought her hand from behind her back. It held one of the books from the table.

"The sacred texts," she said. "There's nothing in them."

"What?"

"The pages. The pages are blank."

Fred took the book. He opened it. A flurry of blank pages flipped beneath his thumb.

"Come," called the Prince from the rooftop outside the window. "Time passes too quickly."

Fred put the book back. He and Rebecca hurried to climb out the window after the Prince. Fred held tight to the staff. Rebecca freed tendrils that the Prince did not seem to know he was trailing. Both of them were thinking hard.

"The sacred texts are blank," said Fred to Rebecca. The Prince was far enough ahead so he would not hear. "They were important to Tarn, but they're blank. What does it mean? It must mean something. It must."

"What we have to think of is what would be in the sacred texts in the first place," said Rebecca.

"Kind of a history, I guess," said Fred. "Rules to live by, laws people made, maybe brave things people have done, good things people have done. Maybe just...stories."

Fred and Rebecca stopped. They looked at each other in understanding.

"We've got to go home," said Fred. "Now. We've got to bring it all here. The manuscript, the notebooks, the slips of paper, the books, all of them. Here. We can't wait for the Great Hall. Grab my hand."

"No," said Rebecca.

"Rebecca! Listen to me. I'm not going to wimp out or

anything. I'll come back. With the notebooks and the manuscript and..."

"We can't both go," said Rebecca. "They'll be looking for us—your dad and my mom and half the apartment building, likely. They'll never let us come back."

"We have to," said Fred.

"I know," said Rebecca. "That's why I'll stay. They'll have to let you come back if I stay."

Fred looked at her. How she could think of everything so fast he didn't know, but he knew she was right. Still, he didn't want to leave her. There were too many things that could go wrong. He didn't even want to think of all the things that could go wrong.

"Rebecca," he began.

"It's all right," she said, hurrying to unhook yet another tendril. "I have to stay, or he'll never make it back to the Great Hall. He'll turn into a tree right here on the roof. Think how unprincely that would be. Hurry up, Fred. You're always late."

She was trying to sound bossy, but it didn't quite come off. For the first time Fred realized that her bossiness was a coverup—Fred had his way of dealing with the uncertainties of life, Rebecca had hers.

"I'll be back," said Fred. "No matter what, I promise I'll be back."

"I know you will," said Rebecca.

She looked at him. For one brief moment they truly understood each other.

Fred raised the golden stick.

"If you please, Staff," he said. "Home."

In the last moment he heard Rebecca calling as if from a great distance.

"Don't worry! I'll be perfectly safe. Remember—nothing exciting ever happens to me!"

Chapter Fourteen

𝒯here was no swirling this time. There was only a great flash of light and Fred was standing in the middle of his apartment. The flash was so bright and the movement so sudden that Fred thought the whole world would know of his arrival, but they did not. For a full twenty seconds the other people in the room were unaware that he was there.

Rebecca was right. They had been missed. Fred's dad was pacing back and forth in front of the balcony windows. Rebecca's mom was sitting white-faced at the dining-room table, with the box and the Tarn papers spread in front of her. Mrs. Tobias was perched on the end of the sofa. A policeman was standing near her taking notes.

"It's like I told Mr. Hamilton," Mrs. Tobias was saying. "I saw the children day before yesterday—in the afternoon. That's when I let them look at this book. Mrs. Hamilton gave it to me. She autographed it, to me, here on the front page."

The policeman didn't seem very interested in the book.

"And then you saw them early yesterday morning?" he asked.

"I didn't see them, I only heard them," said Mrs. Tobias. "When I opened the door..." She turned on the sofa to mime the way she'd opened the door. "Well, my goodness...Fred!"

Everyone turned to look at Fred. His dad took several large steps across the room. Rebecca's mom rose from her chair.

"Wait," said Fred, holding up his hands and the staff as well. "I'm okay. Rebecca's okay too. But there isn't much time."

"What's going on?" asked Fred's dad.

"Where's Rebecca?" asked Rebecca's mom.

"She's with Hisroy," said Fred. "But I've got to get back there fast. Dad, I need everything that was in the box."

Rebecca's mom stepped forward, however, and put her hand on the staff.

"Fred, I have to know. Where is Rebecca?" she asked.

Fred looked at the policeman and at Mrs. Tobias. They were watching with puzzled expressions. He looked at his dad.

"Answer her straight, Fred," said his dad. "She deserves to know."

"Tarn," said Fred. "She's in Tarn."

Rebecca's mom looked across at Fred's dad and then back at Fred.

"Is she in danger?" she asked.

"I don't think so," said Fred. "But I've got to go back and get her. And I have to take the manuscript and notebooks and everything else."

"Why?" asked Rebecca's mom.

"There isn't time. She's all right, but I can't explain it all because there's no time. Please," said Fred.

Rebecca's mom seemed about to protest, then she changed her mind. She began to put the notebooks back in the box. Fred's dad stepped forward and quickly picked up the manuscript, and Fred's mother's plastic pen went rolling across the table. Fred bent forward automatically and caught it as it fell. He slipped it in his pocket.

"I think we need to get a few facts straight here," said the policeman.

Rebecca's mom stepped forward with the box.

"Here it is," she said. "But you can only have it by taking me too."

Fred looked at her in alarm. He looked at his dad. His dad had the manuscript very securely tucked under his arm. Fred didn't know if it was a conspiracy or whether they'd both simply thought of it at the same time. He'd have to take them with him. There wasn't much else he could do.

He looked at the box. Was it all there? All that he needed? No.

"Mrs. Tobias," said Fred. "Your book. I need that too."

"But she gave it to me. I've told you that, Fred..."

"Please, Mrs. Tobias. It's important," said Fred. "It's part of something bigger."

He could see her wavering. Still there was something holding her back.

"Well, she was your mother, but if I let you have it I

wouldn't want to have people poring over it, deciding whether her signature is authentic or not. You know how these things are. People argue and argue about them. I know it was autographed to me and I know she wanted me to have it and I wouldn't want..."

Fred understood.

"You could keep that page," he said. "Tear it out and keep it. You could frame it and put it on your wall."

Mrs. Tobias opened the book. Carefully she eased the fly leaf from the binding. She held the book out to Fred.

"I have a few questions..." began the policeman again.

There was one thing left. It was on the kitchen counter. Fred could see it there. His own copy of *The Prince of Tarn*. He didn't want to give it up. Now, more than ever, he didn't want to give it up. With all that was in the manuscript and the notebooks and Mrs. Tobias's book, wouldn't that be enough? All there was in *The Prince of Tarn*, after all, were trees!

But he couldn't take the chance.

He crossed the room and picked up his own small book. He raised the staff.

His dad and Rebecca's mom encircled him in their arms.

"If you please, Staff," said Fred. "The Great Hall of Tarn."

The policeman was about to take a great leap forward to join them, but Mrs. Tobias grabbed him just in time.

"If I'm not going," she told him firmly, "neither are you."

Chapter Fifteen

$\mathcal{H}$e had been gone no more than ten minutes, but the change in the Great Hall was dramatic. All sorts of vines were winding their way across the high rafters of the hall, flowing down the columns, crossing the marble floor. Everything, even the castle itself, was slipping back into forest.

The Prince was seated on the throne, with Rebecca on the dais beside him. She was pushing back the advancing vines to keep a little area around them clear, but she could do no more for the Prince. His feet had become roots growing into the stone itself. His legs were a tree trunk, thin and slender. His arms and chest and head were still those of the Prince, but they were becoming tree-like too. Tendrils fell from his wrists, elbows and shoulders, encircled his neck and swept through his hair.

Fred's dad and Rebecca's mom stood without moving. Fred took the box and the manuscript and hurried forward.

"Your Highness," said Fred, laying the boxes at the feet of the Prince. "Hisroy, can you hear me?"

The Prince seemed to slowly nod, but he could not speak.

"The Sacred Texts of Tarn," said Fred. "Ezran wouldn't let you read them because there was nothing written in them, the books in the dren are blank."

The Prince's eyes were watching him.

"But there are writings, real writings. Maybe not sacred texts, but a starting place. And they're real. The beginnings of Tarn that we told you about last night. And more too. The names and laws and stories...all written down. I've brought them here. See."

Fred set some of the books in the Prince's lap. He laid one of the Prince's arms across them, the tendrils flowing across the pages.

It seemed to be making no difference. What else could he do? What else was there to do? Could the Prince even really hear him?

"Hisroy!" pressed Fred.

"Maybe it's like he told us," said Rebecca sadly. "Maybe it doesn't matter. He's just a story. What does a story matter?"

Fred looked at Rebecca. Just a story—a story like Hansel and Gretel, or Robin Hood, or Space Invaders from Mars. It was just a story with an unhappy ending, that was all. Had he ever read a story with an unhappy ending?

Yes. Once. And he'd hated it, hated it because...because it was like giving up on yourself. Real life had sad endings sometimes, parts so sad a person could hardly bear it. But stories were somehow meant to be more than that. Stories were something people had invented to give themselves hope.

Was that what his mother had known? Was that why she'd written the Prince so fine and so well?

For a moment it almost seemed clear to Fred. And then it all came crashing down in confusion. All he knew was that, story or no story, the Prince was his friend. He had to find a way to save him.

A long vine was curling, curling across the dais towards the throne. Angrily Fred bent to strike at it. Something jabbed him in the hip.

The pen. It was the small plastic pen with the blue-black ink, the pen that had written the notebooks, the first seeds of Tarn. Fred reached in his pocket. He took it out. It looked so small, so insignificant, but it had written the world of Tarn, it symbolized something larger.

Suddenly Fred knew it wasn't just the Sacred Texts and it wasn't just the past that was missing. The future was missing as well. Standing there, he felt the way he'd felt on his birthday, that night when the Prince had first appeared in his room—all the things that could have been but weren't. Except that wasn't good enough any more. Not for Fred. And not for the Prince of Tarn.

Fred stepped forward and placed the pen in the Prince's hand.

"We have to make things happen, Hisroy," Fred whispered. "I didn't really believe I could before, but I do now. And you can too. I know you can. Everyone's always made things happen for you, but now it's your turn. You've got to write your own story. Maybe you don't even need a pen—maybe all you have to do is live it. But here's the pen, just in case. It's a good one. It worked wonderfully well once. It can again. I know it can, if you want it to."

Very, very slowly the hand seemed to be closing upon that small piece of plastic, closing and closing until it did indeed have the pen in its leafy grasp.

For a long moment everything in the Great Hall was still. Not a vine moved, not a leaf rustled, not an eyelid blinked.

Then a small tree in the corner of the room sneezed.

Fred, Rebecca and his dad and her mom all turned to look. There wasn't a tree there any more. There was a serving girl, hurrying across the Great Hall with a basket of strawberries.

She stopped and blushed and curtsied and said, "Excuse me, Your Highness."

Your Highness! Fred spun around. There, beside him on the dais, stood the Prince. The vines and tendrils were dropping away and he was emerging tall and straight and the look on his face was the look of a thousand conquering princes.

"Guards! Guards!" he cried, and his voice filled the rafters of the Great Hall.

Two guards came in through the front doors, marching smartly. One was tall and lean and had a bearing of pride that almost matched that of the Prince. He didn't know it yet, but he was also missing a button.

"Alert the kitchens," called the Prince. "We have guests in

136

the castle. Have the Stable Master ready his finest horses. Alert the people in the villages. There will be a grand holiday."

"The villages, Your Highness?"

The Prince glanced quickly at Fred.

"I think you'll find that the people have returned," said the Prince. He then spoke once again in tones that rang out through the Great Hall and into the corridors beyond. "Where is Ezran?"

"Here, Your Highness," said a voice from the doorway.

They turned. A figure was standing in the doorway, not a figure old and bent and gnarled as the Prince had described Ezran, but tall and dark-haired, with eyes that flashed in her strong-willed face. Three owls came streaming through the door behind her.

"She's a woman!" Fred said in surprise. "I always thought Ezran was..."

"A man," finished Rebecca. "Oh, Fred—that's what you were supposed to think. That's why the language in the book is so stilted sometimes. Ezran did this. Ezran did that. Never just he or she."

Rebecca's mom had crossed to stand beside them.

"Fred's mother was like that," she said, softly giving them both a hug. "She loved to let you think one way and then turn you on your head and show you how foolish you were."

"And she always wanted to be tall," said Fred's father. "And she always said one day she would dye her hair as black as a raven's feather."

The wizard laughed as she stepped into the room.

"You will have to tell me about this strange woman," she said. "But for now I can only presume that you are the rescuers of our country and, for me, the healers of time itself. Welcome—oh, most welcome—to Tarn."

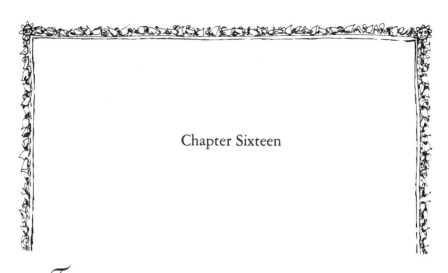

Chapter Sixteen

𝒯hey rode, that day, out upon the lands of Tarn. They dined in the Great Hall. They wandered, in groups large and small, in the gardens or by the water or in the secret rooms of the castle they most wanted to explore.

Fred's dad and Rebecca's mom spent a good deal of time with Ezran the wizard. Fred and Rebecca got to know Garrick, personal bodyguard to the Prince, Cira the serving girl, Aagen the harp player, Rida the cook, and many, many other people of the castle and the villages, as well as enjoying the Prince's company in his own kingdom.

At dusk the Prince went out to the drawbridge to greet his mother and father. They were returning from the outermost reaches of the kingdom, where they had ridden so many years ago to try and help when the woods first began to take over. They themselves had been turned to trees until today. Fred watched the reunion from the parapet just above.

"What do you think, Fred?" asked Rebecca.

She walked over to stand beside him and look down as well. She was dressed in royal robes of blue and gold, was holding a flaming torch and had an owl perched on her shoulder.

"Not bad for someone who never has anything exciting happen to them," said Fred.

"Not me," laughed Rebecca happily. "What do you think of Ferin and Elisia?"

Fred looked down. The man and woman below seemed loving and delightful. Even from a distance, however, it was clear to see, by gesture and by stance, how much the Prince had grown beyond them, how fuller and more human he had become.

"I think they'll learn," said Fred.

The last feast of the evening was held in the open beneath the stars. People had come from across the kingdom, and there were too many even for the Great Hall. It was a wonderful celebration, complete with the hoisting of three banners to a fanfare of trumpets and the light of one hundred torches.

The first banner showed the Royal Eagle of Tarn. On either side were raised two smaller banners of newly sewn silk. One had a background as coppery as Rebecca's hair, the other had lighter, blonder field. On each a young hawk soared its way skyward.

"They didn't have time to do anything fancy," said Aagen, pausing in his harp playing until the trumpets passed. "Still His Royal Highness felt it only proper that you have your own sacred marks of birth to fly beside his own."

As midnight approached, Fred found Ezran gathering them together—Fred, Rebecca, and his dad and her mom. The Prince was there as well. Fred led Ezran quietly aside.

"Does this mean it's time to leave?" asked Fred.

"Yes. Once truly born, Tarn sets out on its own path. Tarn must go its separate way now."

Fred nodded. He was looking closely at Ezran, looking, trying hard to find something...

"I have been told of your mother. She sounds like a remarkable woman. But I am not she," said the wizard.

"She could create all this, but she could not..." Fred was unable to say the words.

"Could not stay with you?"

Fred nodded.

"It is something that you have already proven you understand, Fred," said Ezran. "Life is harder than stories, but the rewards are greater as well."

The Prince had handed Rebecca an owl's feather. Now he brought two to Fred as well.

"The owls gave them willingly," the Prince explained. "It seems that the birds are grateful, as am I."

Fred took the feathers and looked at the Prince questioningly.

"For Jammy," said the Prince. "The second feather is for your friend Jammy. I think he is not really such a bad sort, once given a chance."

No more words needed to be said. Fred smiled at the

Prince. He was going to miss him. A lot.

"What's that noise?" asked Rebecca's mom.

There was indeed a noise. It was a rap, rap, rapping, and then a voice was calling, "Mr. Hamilton? Fred? Rebecca?"

"It's Mrs. Tobias!" said Fred.

"Is that her name?" asked Ezran. "I have heard her calling for years and years in my mind. It was the sound of her voice, and her knocking, that first made me aware there might be someplace safe to send His Royal Highness."

"So Mrs. Tobias *is* a wizard of sorts," said Fred's dad. "An out-of-sorts wizard of sorts."

His dad was the kind of a dad who could tell jokes after all, thought Fred. Well...almost jokes.

"It is time," said Ezran and raised the staff.

"Fred," whispered Rebecca. "I need a pen."

Fred shook his head.

"I need one," said Rebecca.

Fred frowned. Now was not a good time for Rebecca to decide to be bossy again.

"I want to leave my mom's pen here," whispered Fred. "I know the Prince doesn't really need it, but this is where it belongs."

"No, I don't mean I need that pen," whispered Rebecca. "I just need something to write with and a piece of paper. No. Wait."

She looked down at the packed sandy earth at her feet. "I'll write it here. With the feather."

She knelt on the ground and began to write with the

pointed shaft of the owl's feather. Ezran had begun to speak the words of a long and eloquent spell to suit the occasion. Still, there wasn't much time.

Fred saw the words forming themselves on the earth. Yes, he thought. Yes. A story with a good opening line should have a good last line as well. But Rebecca would need his help to finish in time.

He knelt as well. With his own feather he wrote the last three words as Rebecca finished the first part of the phrase.

There was a resounding noise and a great flash. Neither Fred nor Rebecca had time to look up and raise a hand in farewell to the Prince, but they did not regret it. Perhaps, with Hisroy's help, the line they had written upon the earth would come true.

It was a simple line, a line that has been used as long as there have been stories, but a good line still. The writing in the sand read,

And they all lived

happily

ever

after.